THE BOBBSEY TWINS BOOKS

By Laura Lee Hope

THE BOBBSEY TWINS
AND THE HORSESHOE RIDDLE

To Heather
From Auntie Sonia
Christmas 1959.

—

"Let's go down and look carefully"

The Bobbsey Twins and the Horseshoe Riddle

By
LAURA LEE HOPE

Published by
WORLD DISTRIBUTORS (MANCHESTER) LIMITED
LONDON – MANCHESTER
ENGLAND

First impression . . . March 1956
Reprinted . . . . . December 1957
Reprinted . . . . . September 1959

CONTENTS

5

CHAPTER I

A LITTLE BAD LUCK

"DOES a horseshoe really bring good luck, Sam?" Flossie Bobbsey asked, looking up into the face of the kindly coloured man who worked for her father.

"That's what people say, but sometimes——" Sam paused as he took his coat from the kitchen door.

"You mean, Sam, that sometimes it brings *bad* luck?" asked the little boy who was standing beside Flossie. He was Freddie Bobbsey, her twin. They were six years old, had blue eyes, blond curly hair and looked very much alike.

"Well, I really don't know," Sam answered. "Some folks say that if a horseshoe is thrown so it lands with the two ends pointing towards you, that means good luck. But if it lands the other way, with the rounded end towards you, that means bad luck."

Flossie and Freddie thought this over a minute

7

and then asked Sam how he knew so much about horseshoes. The man smiled, showing his fine teeth, and said that he had shod many horses. When he was a young man, Sam said, he used to be a blacksmith.

"Would you like to see a souvenir I've kept all these years?" he asked the children.

"Oh, yes!" they replied together.

"I'll get it," he offered, and went upstairs to the bedroom where he slept in the Bobbsey house.

His wife Dinah, who cooked for the Bobbsey family, turned from the stove where she had just put a batch of cookies in the oven. She smiled at the children and asked:

"What put horseshoes in your pretty heads?"

"A store downtown," Flossie answered.

The little girl explained that a new shop had just been opened. It was a doll and toy-animal hospital, and in the window hung a large horseshoe.

"We saw it on our way home," Freddie added. "We heard somebody say it was supposed to bring good luck to a new business."

"I guess that's right," Dinah agreed. "When folks open up a new store, sometimes their friends send them flowers made in the form of a horse-shoe."

"Next time I have a broken dolly," Flossie said, tossing her curls, "I'll go down to the new store and bring them some good luck."

"And I'll take my broken fire engine," Freddie

added. He loved toy fire-fighting apparatus and had a large collection of them.

At this moment Sam returned, holding a good-sized horseshoe in his hand. He pointed to the seven nails in it, saying that seven was always the number of nails a horseshoe contained.

"If you find one with all seven nails in it, that's supposed to bring you especially good luck," Sam told the children.

"May I play with it?" Freddie asked.

Sam thought a moment. Then he said he would take the seven nails out so they would not be lost, and Freddie might play with the horseshoe in the back yard.

"I'll fix up a little space and you can play horseshoes," Sam offered.

He led the way to the back yard and hammered a little wooden stake into the ground. Then he stepped back and tossed the horseshoe. *Plop!* It landed with a soft thud right around the stake.

"Well, I had a little luck." He grinned. "Now you try it."

Freddie took a turn first. He found the horseshoe rather heavy and could not throw it far. Sam told him to move closer. Freddie did so, and this time the horseshoe landed directly over the peg.

"That's fine," said Sam, and then returned to the house.

"I want a turn," Flossie begged.

She picked up the horseshoe and tossed it. But

it did not come close to the peg. The little girl was about to skip over and get the horseshoe when a twelve-year-old boy ran into the yard. He was Danny Rugg.

"What are you doing?" he asked, grabbing up the horseshoe.

Freddie and Flossie did not like Danny. He was always playing tricks on the younger children, and the little twins had a feeling that Danny might try one right now. They ran off a little way in order to avoid him.

"Only sissies stand so close to the peg," Danny said, and walked backwards towards the garage.

Tossing the horseshoe high, Danny flung it way past the peg and almost at Flossie's feet. The little girl looked down at it. Then she exclaimed:

"Danny! You've brought me bad luck!"

"What do you mean?" he asked.

Flossie pointed. The horseshoe lay with the rounded end towards her. She repeated what Sam had told the twins a little while before.

Danny laughed loudly. He picked up the horseshoe and threw it again. This time it landed in front of Freddie in the same position.

"I hope you have bad luck, too!" Danny cried and ran out of the yard.

"He's the meanest boy in Lakeport!" Flossie stamped her foot. "Oh, Freddie, do you suppose we're both going to have bad luck?"

As Freddie stood looking at the horseshoe, the

children's older brother and sister came into the yard. They were twins also, but did not look like Freddie and Flossie. Bert and Nan were tall for their twelve years, and had dark hair and brown eyes.

"Why was Danny running away from here?" Bert asked curiously.

Flossie explained about the horseshoe and how Danny had brought bad luck to her and Freddie.

"You shouldn't listen to things like that," said Nan. She walked up and put her arms around the younger twins. "That's just superstition and doesn't mean a thing," she said.

"But how about the good luck?" Flossie asked. "Won't we have that either?"

Nan laughed. "Yes, I'm sure you will."

"Say," said Bert, "how would you two like to go riding with Nan and me?"

Freddie asked what kind of a ride Bert meant. Upon learning that he meant horseback riding, the little boy was eager to go, and Flossie, too, said she wanted to ride on a Shetland pony.

"I'll ask Mother," said Bert, "and get some money."

He went into the house and returned in a few minutes. Mrs. Bobbsey had given her permission; so the four children, wearing dungarees and sweaters, set off for Chris Ridgeway's riding academy some distance from their home. It was located at the edge of a wood which had beautiful trails for horseback riders.

"I hope he has that lovely palomino they call Bessie," said Nan. "I had lots of fun riding her last time I was there."

"And I like that black horse Prince," said Bert. "It's neat the way he trots."

Freddie and Flossie had never been to the riding academy. But they had heard from other children that its Shetland ponies were gentle and fun to ride. Half an hour later the twins reached the stable and went into Chris Ridgeway's office. He was just finishing a telephone call. Putting down the telephone, he looked at the Bobbseys and smiled.

"I brought my brother Freddie and my sister Flossie," Bert spoke up. "Have you two Shetland ponies they can ride?"

"I sure have," Chris replied. "Have you children ever ridden before?"

"Oh, yes," said Flossie and Freddie together, and Freddie added, "We were out West one time and rode ponies."

"That's fine," said Chris. "I'll take you into the woods."

"Goody!" Flossie cried, clapping her hands and feeling very grown-up to be allowed on a trail the older people used.

Chris took them into the stable and Nan and Bert at once found the ponies they wanted. Bessie nuzzled Nan, and the girl was sure the lovely pony remembered her. Bert led Prince out of his stall and asked if he might saddle him.

"Sure, go ahead," Chris replied.

He brought two adorable-looking Shetland ponies for Freddie and Flossie. Flossie's was almost pure white with only a trace of brown markings. Freddie's was black with a white nose and tail.

Chris lifted the small twins into the saddles and adjusted the stirrup straps. Then he helped Nan and Bert. When the twins were ready, he climbed on to his own beautiful roan mare and the little group set off.

The woods were beautiful in the sunny summer afternoon. The children enjoyed watching the birds flitting from tree to tree and squirrels and rabbits scurrying through the underbrush.

The riders jogged along for about twenty minutes, then Chris decided they should go back. They turned, and now Freddie and Flossie led the procession. When they were about ten minutes away from the stables, the quiet of the woods was suddenly disturbed.

BANG! The riders sat up very straight, looking around. The noise had sounded like several giant cap pistols going off at once. It had frightened the ponies, whose ears first had stood up straight and now were pressed tightly back against their heads.

The next instant—BOOM! There was another explosion. This was too much for Flossie's and Freddie's ponies. They dashed off along the trail. The children, swaying from side to side, tried desperately to hold on.

CHAPTER II

HORSESHOE LODGE

"WHOA!" Chris shouted at the runaway ponies.

The Shetland which Flossie was riding stopped galloping and slowed down to a trot. But Freddie's pony paid no attention. He seemed to be going faster than ever.

Freddie had often been in trouble before, but fortunately he had always been saved just in time. Nan, Bert and Flossie had had their share of exciting experiences too. Some of these had been in Lakeport where they lived, and others at the many interesting places to which their parents had taken them.

They had been to the seashore, to farms, on ranches, and to camp. Recently they had had a most exciting adventure AT WHITESAIL HARBOUR, where Bert entered his midget speedboat in a race and they all solved a mystery about another boat.

But right now Nan and Bert were very much

14

frightened about Freddie on the runaway pony. They urged their own ponies to run faster, but realized in a moment that they could not possibly catch Freddie's.

Chris, meanwhile, slapped his horse on the rump and galloped at a mad pace after the runaway.

"Whoa! Whoa!" he shouted again.

Freddie's excited pony raced on, but Chris's horse caught up to it in a few moments. Reaching out an arm, Chris swept Freddie off the pony and planted the little boy directly in front of him in the saddle.

"Hang on!" he ordered.

Freddie clung tightly to the edge of the big saddle. As he watched, Chris kept pace with the Shetland. Presently the man grabbed the pony's reins and pulled hard on them. In a few seconds the pony slowed down and trotted alongside the big horse as far as the stable.

Chris jumped down and lifted Freddie to the ground. The poor little boy was shaking with fright. In fact, he was too frightened to speak. Chris patted him on the shoulder, saying kindly:

"I'm mighty glad you didn't fall off. I wonder who made that noise back in the woods. If I could find out who did it, I'd certainly go after him and give the fellow a piece of my mind."

By this time the other Bobbseys had ridden up, very relieved that their brother had not been hurt. Nan also spoke of the noise that had made the ponies run away, and asked Chris what he thought it was. But the riding master said he did not know what it could have been.

Suddenly he noticed that Prince was limping. Examining his hoof, Chris discovered that the pony had thrown a shoe. Bert said it must have come off when Prince started to run, because the pony had stumbled a little after that.

"We're just having all kinds of bad luck," exclaimed Flossie.

She told Chris Ridgeway how Danny Rugg had thrown the horseshoe so it had landed with the rounded end towards the small twins. Chris smiled, and said she should not be worried by this, even though Freddie had come pretty close to having an accident.

"Besides, nothing happened to you, Flossie," he added.

Flossie looked up at him. Then she said very solemnly, "Anything that happens to Freddie is just like happening to me. I'm his twin, you know."

"If that's the case, then I'm twice as glad Freddie didn't fall off the pony," Chris replied. Then he said that the only time he had ever heard of horseshoes bringing bad luck was in connection with an old hotel in the town of Bartley, several miles from Lakeport.

"Tell us about it," Freddie begged.

"Well, this Bartley Lodge," Chris began, "was built at the time of the Revolutionary War. It was a place where stage-coaches changed horses on their long trips."

As Chris paused, Nan asked him what horseshoes had to do with the old place. Chris said that from Revolutionary times on, the various owners of the place had collected horseshoes worn by famous horses or by horses belonging to famous people.

"I believe there's one shoe there from Paul Revere's horse," he said. "But the place had plenty of bad luck. Once there was a fire, another time a tornado took the roof off, and finally, a few years ago, the lodge was condemned."

"What does that mean?" Flossie asked.

"That the owner couldn't let people stay there any more because the building was not safe," Chris explained. "Old Mr. Dickson felt very bad about it. After the authorities made him close up his place, he moved into a small wing at one end, and lived there until the time of his death about eight months ago."

Since then, all sorts of stories had been circulating about the old lodge, Chris added. One story was that a ghost was haunting the lodge. Another was that every once in a while a horseshoe would fall off the wall for apparently no reason at all.

"I understand that there is some other mystery in connection with the place, too," Chris said, "but I can't recall what it is."

The twins were excited about the story and were

sorry that Chris Ridgeway could not remember what this other mystery was. But he said he must leave now, and see about having another shoe put on Prince's foot.

"Do you want his old shoe if I can find it?" Bert asked him.

"No. We always put new ones on our horses when we shoe them," Chris replied.

Bert Bobbsey decided to go back into the woods and look for the horseshoe anyway. He would keep it as a souvenir.

The other children walked along the trail with him. They glanced left and right and ahead, hoping to find the shoe, but they did not see it.

"Maybe the person who made the noise and scared the ponies took it," Nan suggested.

The twins walked on for several more minutes without locating the horseshoe. Finally Bert declared that they were back at the spot where they had heard the noise and the ponies had run away.

"I'm sure Prince lost the shoe somewhere between here and the stable," he said. "I guess we'd better give up."

"Maybe Chris Ridgeway will give you another horseshoe," Freddie suggested.

The twins returned to the stable and Bert asked the riding master for one. But Chris did not have any horseshoes in the place. He said his ponies were always taken to a blacksmith's to be shod.

"Prince is already over at the one on Spring Street," he said. "If you go there, I'm sure the smith will give you a shoe."

"Did Prince wear any special kind of horseshoe?" Bert asked.

"Well," Chris said, "not exactly special. But there was a star imprinted on his shoe."

"I see," Bert said. "If we get over to the blacksmith's, I'll ask him to give me the shoe with the star on it."

The children walked home and were just in time to meet their father going into the house. The tall good-looking man said hello to them all, then picked Flossie up in his arms.

"Well, what's my Fat Fairy been doing today?" he asked.

Flossie giggled. Since she had been a tiny baby, her father had called her Fat Fairy, and she loved the nickname.

"Fat Fairy has been riding on a lovely pony," the little girl reported. "And Danny threw a horseshoe at us. And we've had bad luck and we might have more bad luck," she said.

"Wait a minute!" Mr. Bobbsey laughed. "What's all this about?"

The four children took turns telling him just what had happened during the afternoon. At the end of the story he smiled, and said they should not take any of it too seriously. Turning to Freddie, he declared:

"I know my Little Fireman isn't afraid of horse-shoes that are turned the wrong way."

"Of course not," said Freddie manfully.

Mrs. Bobbsey came downstairs and kissed her husband. She was a charming, pretty woman, and the twins loved her dearly.

Presently the family went to the dinner table. After grace had been said and they had started to eat, Mr. Bobbsey remarked that he was going to take a little business trip. He owned a large lumber concern on Lake Metoka, which lay alongside Lakeport.

"I'm going over to Bartley to see a man who makes plywood," he said.

"Please, may we go with you?" Flossie asked.

Mr. Bobbsey smiled. "I was thinking about taking the whole family," he said. "There's to be a big celebration in Bartley in connection with the 175th anniversary of the founding of the town. I believe you would enjoy seeing the parade and all the things that they are going to have on display there."

Freddie gave a whoop. "That's where the haunted Horseshoe Lodge is," he said excitedly. "We can go and see it!"

Flossie looked across the table at her twin. She gave a little shiver as she said:

"You mean, Freddie, you *want* to see a ghost?"

CHAPTER III

A LOST INVITATION

"WHAT'S all this about a ghost?" Mrs. Bobbsey asked, laughing.

The children repeated the story Chris Ridgeway had told about the deserted old hotel in Bartley, which Freddie had called Horseshoe Lodge.

"It does sound spooky," their mother admitted. "It might be fun to see the place at that," she added, looking at her husband.

Mr. Bobbsey laughed too, and said if they went to Bartley they would surely go around to see the old lodge.

"When can we leave?" Flossie asked. "To-morrow?"

"Not that soon, Fat Fairy," her father replied. "I have a few things to take care of early next week, but we'll start shortly after that."

Flossie held up one hand and began to count on her fingers. "Today is Saturday," she said, pushing down one finger. "And tomorrow is Sunday," she added, pushing down another finger. "And we won't go Monday," she sighed, with three fingers turned down now. She looked up at her father and smiled. "Maybe it will be Tuesday?" she asked.

"You're a little tease," Mr. Bobbsey said. "But I'm afraid it can't be that soon."

Nan wanted to go to Bartley very much, but she was glad they would not leave until after Nellie Parks' party. Nellie was giving it on Monday for a cousin who was visiting her. The guests were to attend a special play for older children at the Lakeport Theatre.

"We're invited to lunch, first," Nan told her mother Monday noon, as she started to dress for the party.

"That's very nice," Mrs. Bobbsey smiled.

Nan put on a pretty green silk dress with white collar and cuffs, then walked down the street towards the Parks' home. On the way she met Grace Lavine and Helen Porter.

"Hello, Nan," they said together. "Where's Bert?"

"I don't know," Nan replied. "I think he went to fly his model plane."

"Isn't he coming to the party?" Grace asked.

"Was he supposed to?" Nan asked, looking at Grace in surprise.

"Yes. Didn't he get an invitation?"

"No," Nan replied. "I didn't think there were going to be any boys at the party."

"Why, sure, boys were invited," Helen Porter replied.

Nan was amazed. When she reached Nellie's house, four boys and three girls were playing games in the back yard with Nellie.

"Hi!" Nan said. "Nellie, did you invite Bert to this party?"

"Why, yes," Nellie said. "Didn't he get my invitation?"

"I'm sure he didn't," Nan answered. "He certainly would have told me about it."

"Oh, dear," said Nellie. "I sent separate invitations to you in the mail. I thought it was funny I hadn't heard from Bert. Well, let's get him right away."

"But I can't," said Nan in dismay. "He's gone off and I don't know where he is."

"But we have to do something," said Nellie. "I have theatre tickets for everybody. And it's a good show too."

Nan said she would try to find her twin. Hurrying to the telephone, she called her mother, but Mrs. Bobbsey had no idea where Bert was, although she was sure he was not far away.

"What'll I do?" thought Nan.

As she hung up, Nan noticed a girl whom she had never seen before coming down the stairs. The girl smiled, saying she was Joy Lambert, Nellie's cousin.

"I'll bet she's loads of fun," Nan told herself, as

she looked at the pretty girl's short black hair and twinkling eyes. She was tall and slender and Nan was sure she was an athlete.

The girls went out to the back yard together, and Nellie introduced Joy to her other guests. Then Nan told how she was looking for Bert. At once his friend Charlie Mason said:

"Let's start a search. We'll divide up in teams."

Overhearing this, Mrs. Parks said she would give them half an hour to find Bert. By that time they must be back to lunch or they would be late for the theatre.

"We'll make it a game," Nellie called out. "First team to find Bert in half an hour gets a prize!"

What a quick exit there was, with each team hoping to win! Nan had chosen Joy for a partner.

"Let's go down to the park and look," Nan said. "Bert likes to fly his model plane near the pond."

Charlie Mason and Phil Moore had the same idea, and the four arrived there at the same time. Bert was not in sight.

"Ten minutes gone," said Joy. "Where do we go next?"

"To Lake Metoka near my father's lumber-yard," Nan whispered.

But again the boys had the same thought. This time they reached the spot first and started looking.

"Hey, there he is!" Charlie shouted, just as the girls ran up. "Bert, come here quick!"

As Bert hurried from the shore, Nan and Joy

dashed up. Laughing, Nan said to Charlie and Phil:

"You win. But you'd better hurry if you want the prize. There's not much time left!"

"Say, what's this all about?" Bert asked.

"Can't tell you now. Follow us!" Charlie answered.

He and Phil just made it back to Nellie's in the eight minutes that were left. Both boys received a book for a prize, and now Bert heard the reason for the mad dash.

"I didn't get your invitation, Nellie," he said. "But I'm glad to be here."

Mrs. Parks said luncheon was on the table and they must sit down at once.

"Joy lives in Bartley," Nellie told her guests as they were eating. "There's going to be a big celebration in her town next week. Tell us about it, Joy."

Her cousin described the 175th anniversary parade and exhibits. When she finished, Nan said:

"We're going to see them."

"Oh, that's wonderful," said Joy. "Be sure to get in touch with me."

"Have you ever seen the old lodge there?" Nan asked her. "We've heard it's very spooky—has a ghost and everything."

"That's right," Joy answered. "They say the place is full of funny doors and secret rooms."

"Can you get inside the lodge now?" Nan asked.

"Sure," said Joy. "A caretaker lives in the wing where old Mr. Dickson used to live. He'll show you around."

"Say, Nan," said Charlie Mason, "I heard Freddie's pony ran away with him. Did he get hurt?"

"No," Nan replied. Then she asked, "Did you hear about the noise that scared his pony?"

"Yes. Do you know what made it?"

Nan explained that no one had any idea, but the sound was like an explosion. Charlie said the same thing had happened several times since and had frightened several other horses.

"I'll bet I know who did it," Nellie remarked.

"Who?" everyone asked.

"Danny Rugg," Nellie replied. "I saw him the other day with some toy bombs. He was hiding behind a hedge and throwing them at people as they passed by."

"The noise did sound like a bomb going off," Nan admitted. "As soon as the play's over this afternoon, let's go to Danny's house, Bert, and find out."

"Sure thing," her twin agreed.

The party of children hurried off to the theatre. They spent the afternoon laughing at the adventures of two boys, one a cowboy, the other from New York, who exchanged places. The cowboy insisted upon walking with his dogie on the city streets. The city boy took his roller skates to the ranch. What spills he had using them on the rough prairie land!

"Oh, that was wonderful!" declared Nan, as the curtain fell at the play's end.

As she and her twin left the theatre, Nan whispered, "Now, Bert, let's go and talk to Danny Rugg."

"Good idea," Bert agreed.

After thanking Nellie for giving them such a nice time, Bert and Nan set off for Danny's house. They caught sight of him in his back yard and walked up to the boy.

"Listen, Danny," said Bert, "did you set off a toy bomb in the woods and scare my brother's pony?"

"You nearly made Freddie fall off and hurt himself," Nan added indignantly.

"I did not!" Danny cried out. "Anyway, you're a bunch of sissies, you Bobbseys."

Knowing Bert would try to get even for this remark, Danny ran up on the back porch of his home. Taking something from his pocket, he threw it directly at the twins.

BANG! It was a toy bomb that landed in front of them and exploded. The gravel inside the bomb flew up at Bert and Nan, stinging their faces and arms.

"Oh!" Nan cried out, rubbing her cheek.

Bert raced towards Danny. He wasn't going to let him get away with this! But the proposed fight took a strange turn. As Danny turned to run into the house, he suddenly shouted:

"Better run, Bert Bobbsey! The police are after you!"

Danny pointed along the driveway. Bert looked up. Sure enough, a policeman was walking swiftly towards Bert!

CHAPTER IV

STICKY BUSINESS

"SO you're the boy who's been causing all the trouble in Lakeport recently," the policeman said in a stern voice to Bert Bobbsey.

"No, sir, I'm not the one," Bert answered, astonished. He did not recognize the policeman, although he knew several of the men on the force.

The officer eyed what was left of the bomb. Paper, gravel and bits of string lay on the grass.

"My twin didn't do that!" Nan spoke up.

"Well, if you didn't do it," the policeman said, turning to Bert, "who did?"

Nan and Bert looked at each other. They did not want to tattle on Danny. Noticing their hesitation, the officer looked Bert straight in the eye.

"You act guilty," he said. "If you won't tell me who's responsible for these scares, you'd better come along with me."

"You mean to the police station?" Nan exclaimed. "Oh, no, please!"

The policeman gazed down at her worried face. Then suddenly he smiled. "You just mentioned you were twins, didn't you?" he asked.

When Nan nodded, he said to Bert, "Then you aren't Danny Rugg."

The twins laughed in relief, realizing now that it was Danny the officer had come to see. They were glad they had not told on him. Now Danny could not call them squealers. He had a habit of doing this whenever he was caught.

The policeman asked the twins their names, then said:

"I'm glad you had nothing to do with frightening the horses in the woods. Just this morning another bomb went off and frightened a horse. Chris Ridgeway has lodged a complaint with the police. We heard that Danny Rugg has been seen playing with toy bombs lately, so I came to talk to him."

The officer went up the porch steps and knocked on the door. As Bert and Nan started off, they could hear Danny shouting at the top of his voice that he knew nothing about what had happened in the woods.

"He'd never admit it anyhow," Bert said to Nan. "He'd be too scared."

As Nan and Bert walked into their own back yard, they saw Flossie playing with her dolls. Flossie had a large collection of them, but the most beautiful was Jean. The doll was blonde, blue-eyed and curly-haired, and looked very much like

Flossie. The little girl had taken very good care of Jean because she was breakable.

With Flossie and the dolls were the Bobbseys' two dogs. Old Snap, large and shaggy, was lying in the sun asleep. Waggo, the young fox terrier, was frisking around, barking.

"Waggo's doing tricks to entertain my dolls," Flossie explained to her older brother and sister.

She made a circle of her arms and Waggo jumped through them.

"Good dog!" she said. "Now do a somersault!"

Waggo obeyed, then jumped up, wagging his tail. Next Flossie held out a stick for him to leap over. He did this trick very nicely, too.

She moved a little distance away and held the stick up higher. Waggo nimbly jumped over it. But this time he landed directly on top of Snap! The old dog growled and rose angrily. He started for Waggo.

"Now, don't fight," Flossie commanded fearfully. "Waggo couldn't help it, Snap." She patted the old dog and after a few yips at the terrier, he lay down again and closed his eyes.

At this moment Freddie came from the house. Seeing Waggo in a frisky mood, he began to chase him around the yard. Waggo loved this. The children had trained the terrier to leap into the air, twist his body around, and land on all four feet. Now Freddie urged him to do this, and Waggo performed over and over to the delight of all the twins. The little dog became very excited, and in his glee he suddenly grabbed Jean by the hair and shook her violently.

"Waggo! You stop that!" Flossie cried, dashing over to rescue her doll. "You'll break her!"

Waggo was having too much fun to stop. He raced around the yard, swinging Jean between his teeth. Suddenly the doll flew from his mouth and landed against the trunk of an apple tree.

"Oh, my baby!" Flossie shrieked and ran to pick up the doll. "She's hurt!" the little girl cried.

Nan rushed over to see what had happened. Poor Jean's head had broken off across the forehead!

Tears came to Flossie's eyes. Her lovely doll would never be the same again! Nan put her arm around her little sister and said:

"If we take Jean down to the new doll hospital, maybe she can be mended."

Flossie brightened and early the next morning put Jean's body and the top of her head into a box. Carrying it under her arm, she started downtown with Nan. When they reached the doll hospital, Flossie pointed out the horseshoe which was hanging in the window.

"I hope the toy mender can bring good luck to Jean," she said.

Nan noticed that, neatly printed in one corner of the window, were the words: DICKSON TOY-MENDING SHOP. She suddenly remembered that the former owner of Horseshoe Lodge had been a man named Dickson. Nan wondered if the two men could have been relatives.

When the twins went inside the shop, a pleasant but rather sad-looking young man walked towards the children and told them he was Mr. Dickson.

"I'd like my dolly mended," said Flossie, opening the box.

Mr. Dickson examined Jean and said he thought he could fix her so the crack would not even show.

"I have some glue here which I invented myself," he explained. "Anything that's mended with it will never come apart."

"You mean other things besides toys?" Flossie asked him.

Mr. Dickson said the glue would mend anything —wood, plastic and even metals of all kinds.

"May I buy some?" Nan wanted to know, thinking her mother might like to have some.

"I haven't made enough of it to sell yet," Mr. Dickson replied. "I invented it to mend my own little girl's toys. I'm really a chemist, but the doctor made me give up that kind of work."

"What a shame!" Nan remarked. "Is that why you opened this shop?"

"Yes," Mr. Dickson said. "My wife was helping me here. But now she's in the hospital, and my little girl is, too."

"Oh, what happened to them?" Flossie asked.

Mr. Dickson explained that they had been badly hurt in a motoring accident.

"They'll be laid up for some time," he sighed.

Nan and Flossie felt sorry for him and were about to say so, when he went on, "I ought to patent the formula for this new glue, and make a lot of it to sell. But I haven't any money to manufacture the glue. It takes all I can earn here to pay our bills."

"What's *patent-the-formula*?" Flossie asked curiously.

Mr. Dickson smiled at the little girl. "A formula is like a recipe," he explained. "I ought to write down the recipe for making my glue, and give a copy of the recipe to the Government to hold. Then no one else would have the right to make glue the way I make mine. That's called taking out a patent," he added. Then suddenly he shook off his unhappy mood, saying he should not bother two such nice little girls with his troubles. He would mend the doll at once.

Reaching up to a shelf, he took down a can. He set it on the counter, then picked up a tiny paint brush. Very carefully he smeared the colourless glue along the broken edges of Jean's head. Skilfully he placed her forehead against the rest of her face and held it firm.

"In a few minutes," Mr. Dickson said, "this glue will set so hard that your doll's head will never come apart again."

Flossie leaned far over the counter and kept her eyes fixed on the doll. As she watched, the crack gradually seemed to disappear. The little girl clapped her hands in joy.

"Jean's mended!" she exclaimed happily.

No one had noticed that as Flossie bent down, her curls were getting closer and closer to the can of glue. Presently one of them dipped down into it. When she raised her head, the curl plastered itself against the back of her dress. But Nan and Mr. Dickson still did not notice.

"Perhaps you'd like to look around the shop a bit," Mr. Dickson suggested. "I'd like this glue to get good and hard before you take your doll home."

Nan and Flossie walked around looking at the various dolls and toys. Flossie picked up a jointed monkey which had been brought in to have its tail put back on. Suddenly she felt something tug at her hair.

"Ouch!" she said aloud.

Since no one was standing near her, she wondered who had pulled her hair. When she turned her head the hair was yanked again. Putting up a hand, the little girl suddenly discovered that one curl was stuck tight to her dress.

Nan had walked over to see why Flossie had cried out. Now she discovered the reason. "Goodness," she told Flossie, "I can't get your curl loose!"

"Oh, no!" the little girl wailed. "I'll be stuck up all the rest of my life!"

CHAPTER V

"I GUESS we'll have to cut your curl off, Flossie," Nan said. "And I don't know what will happen to your dress."

"But I don't want my curl cut off," Flossie objected. "I'll look funny with part of my hair gone."

They rushed over to Mr. Dickson to see what he could do about getting the glue off. The young man was just lifting the can of glue up to a shelf. He turned quickly, his hand slipped off the can, and down it toppled, spilling the contents on all three of them!

"Oo—ee!" Flossie wailed.

Nan grabbed a cloth she saw under the counter and tried to wipe Flossie's hair. But the glue had already started to harden and would not come off. The pungent odour made them all sneeze.

Flossie began to cry. "I'm going home!" she sobbed, running towards the door. "I'll get my mother to take this out of my hair!"

"No, come back!" Mr. Dickson begged her. "Your mother can never get it out. Wait! I'll think of something."

Then, talking more to himself than to the girls, and grabbing several bottles from his workbench, he muttered:

"I mustn't put on anything that will burn. And it mustn't take the colour out either."

The chemist snatched up a small bowl into which he poured liquids from three different bottles. Then he sprinkled in some powder from a box. Stirring the mixture quickly with a stick, he said:

"I'll try this on the ends of your hair. If it doesn't work, you can cut the ends off."

Flossie was too frightened to have the experiment tried on her. But Nan stood quietly as Mr. Dickson daubed the ends of her hair with the solution. He watched closely for a few seconds, then a smile came over his face. The glue was actually turning back to a liquid. With some cheesecloth the chemist wiped it off. Nan's hair had not been harmed!

"Thank goodness," Mr. Dickson said. "Now I'll take off all this glue before it hardens any more."

In a few minutes there was no trace of it on any of them. But the chemist advised the girls to hurry home and have shampoos as quickly as possible.

When Mr. Bobbsey heard the story at lunchtime, he became very much interested. He asked several questions, getting all the details about the glue and also the mixture that dissolved it.

"That glue is something builders have been looking for a long time," he said. "And the dissolvent could do wonders and should be patented immediately."

Nan told him how Mr. Dickson had had to give up his position as a chemist because of his health. Now he was so discouraged and worried about his family that he was not bothering with his invention.

"That's too bad," said Mr. Bobbsey. "I'd like to help him. Nan, suppose you and I go down after lunch and talk to him."

"Yes, let's," his daughter said eagerly.

When they reached Mr. Dickson's shop, Nan introduced her father. At first the chemist was afraid Mr. Bobbsey had come to complain about the accident. The young man was relieved when he found that Mr. Bobbsey wanted to talk about how the glue could be used in the manufacture of plywood and similar products.

"I understand you haven't patented it yet," Mr. Bobbsey said.

"No, I haven't," Mr. Dickson admitted, "and I suppose I should. Well, I'll think it over."

"I'll be very glad to help you," Mr. Bobbsey offered.

"Thank you," said Mr. Dickson. "I'll let you know."

After Mr. Bobbsey left, the chemist continued to talk to Nan. He told her that an uncle of his who had died a few months before had left him a good sum of money, which would have helped him manufacture the glue.

"But I'll probably never get it," he sighed.

"Why? Did your uncle change his mind about leaving you the money?" Nan asked him.

"No one knows. My uncle left a strange will," Mr. Dickson replied. "I was named as his heir, but his money has not been found. My uncle was a rather odd person. After Bartley Lodge was con-demned——"

"Was the owner your uncle?" Nan exclaimed.

"Yes," Mr. Dickson said, and continued:

"My uncle asked me to help him seal up every shutter and door in the old part of the hotel. I had just invented my glue and thought it would be a good chance to try it out. It worked all right. Only an earthquake could get those doors loose!" Then he added, "Except possibly my new dis-solvent."

"And you think the missing money is hidden somewhere in the lodge?" Nan asked Mr. Dickson.

"No, I don't." After a pause he went on, "The lawyers thought that my uncle probably buried it somewhere."

"Didn't he leave any clue?" Nan questioned eagerly.

"No, not one," Mr. Dickson replied. "So that's

the story and I still haven't any money to start a manufacturing business."

Nan told him that her family was going to Bartley soon to see the 175th anniversary celebration. They hoped to visit what her small brother called Horseshoe Lodge and look around.

"Well, if you find the hidden money," Mr. Dickson said, smiling, "I'll be very grateful to you." As an afterthought he said suddenly, "Say, this would be a fine chance to try out my dissolvent on something that's been stuck with the glue for several months. Would you like to take some of it with you and see if it will open one of the doors?"

Nan did not feel that she should agree without speaking to her mother and father about it. She said she would let Mr. Dickson know the answer.

"Well, if they'll let you, come for a bottle of the dissolvent just before you go to Bartley," the chemist requested.

Nan consented and left the store. Upon reaching home, she met Freddie and Flossie, who were on their way to Mr. Dickson's shop.

"We have to pick up Jean," the little girl said.

The small twins' arms were full of broken toys. Freddie was carrying a set of miniature soldiers. A leg was gone from one, another had lost his rifle, and still another had come apart so that his shoes were separated from the rest of his body. Under Freddie's other arm was his broken fire engine. Flossie was lugging a doll's bed.

"I'm going to be a glue-mending man when I grow up," Freddie announced to Nan.

She laughed. "I thought you wanted to be a fireman."

"I can be both," said Freddie. "When there aren't any fires, I'll mend toys."

The small twins ran off and in a little while reached the doll and toy hospital. Just before they went inside, Freddie dropped one of his soldiers. As he stooped to pick it up, and Flossie waited for him, the two children heard a man's angry voice inside the store:

"I want that glue formula, Dickson. Give it to me or you'll get hurt!"

CHAPTER VI

THE OLD STAGE-COACH

FREDDIE and Flossie looked at each other, their hearts pounding in fright. Someone inside Mr. Dickson's shop was threatening him!

"We'd better get a policeman," Flossie suggested.

"We haven't time," Freddie replied. "Look! That man is shaking his fist at Mr. Dickson. Maybe he really will hit him."

"But we have to help Mr. Dickson somehow," Flossie insisted. "What'll we do?"

Freddie thought for a second. Then he had an idea. "Let's play fire!"

"How?" his twin asked.

"I'll be a fireman inside and you be one outside," Freddie directed. "You stay here and do just what I do."

With this he started yelling, "Fire! Fire!" at the top of his voice and rushed inside the shop.

Flossie took up the cry on the sidewalk. "Fire! Fire!" she shrieked at the top of her voice.

The stranger inside the shop looked at Freddie and then dashed towards the door.

"Where's the fire?" he asked.

Freddie pointed vaguely out-of-doors. When the man heard Flossie scream, he dashed from the shop to ask her.

Mr. Dickson had come from behind the counter and started to rush outside also. But Freddie held him back.

"Don't go!" he begged, and held tightly to the toy mender's coat.

At this second Flossie scooted past the stranger and into the shop. Freddie slammed the door shut and the lock snapped. The stranger came back and shook the door-knob, but could not open the door.

"You're a bad man!" Flossie called to him. "You can't come in."

Mr. Dickson looked at Freddie in surprise. "There isn't any fire?" he asked.

Freddie grinned. "I guess maybe there's one some place," he said. "But we just didn't want that man to hurt you."

Suddenly Mr. Dickson realized that the children had been helping him. He put his arms around the twins' shoulders and said:

"Thank you very much for getting rid of Will Hemp for me."

The stranger, who had been standing outside the door all this time, glared at the group inside the store. He shook his finger at them and then turned to leave. Flossie thought what an ugly man he was and noticed he had a crooked red scar on his forehead.

"Do you have a back door?" Freddie asked suddenly. "If you do, you'd better lock it, Mr. Dickson."

The chemist patted Freddie's shoulder and said he was glad to be reminded of this. He walked through a rear room of his shop and locked a door which led into an alleyway. When he came back, Mr. Dickson said to the twins:

"I suppose I should explain to you about Will Hemp. We both lived in Bartley when we were boys. He was never any good.

"Several years ago he and I tried working on

some experiments together in the school lab. One
of them had to do with glue. Recently Will found
out about my glue and came here to threaten me.
He said it was he who really had invented it."

"But he didn't, did he?" Freddie asked.

"Of course not," Mr. Dickson replied.

He admitted that the incident had given him a
real scare, however, and said he would be glad to
have Mr. Bobbsey take care of having the formula
patented.

"Please go and see Daddy right now, before that
mean Mr. Hemp comes back," Flossie urged him.

The chemist looked at the little girl and said he
thought this would be a smart thing to do. Would
the twins like to go with him?

"Yes, we would," Flossie replied. "But first I
want to get my doll that I forgot."

"And here are some toys to be mended," added
Freddie, who was still holding the fire engine and
the broken soldiers.

Mr. Dickson said he would fix them later in the
day and Freddie could get the toys the next
morning.

The three of them left the shop and the twins
showed their new friend the way to Mr. Bobbsey's
lumber-yard.

"It's the best lumber-yard in the world," Freddie
said proudly.

"Yes, it is," Flossie agreed. "And Daddy is the
best daddy in all the world, too."

"I think," said Mr. Dickson, smiling, "that your daddy is just about the luckiest man in the world to have twins like you."

They walked into Mr. Bobbsey's office and Mr. Dickson explained what the children had done and how he was now convinced that he ought to have the glue formula patented.

"I'm glad you came," the twins' father said, smiling. "I have a friend who is a patent lawyer. I'll see him today and he will arrange everything for you."

Mr. Dickson took two papers from his pocket, on which the formulas were written, and handed them to Mr. Bobbsey.

"I appreciate this more than I can tell you," the young man said.

He and the twins left the lumber office and walked up the street. Presently he said to them, "I understand you're going to Bartley for the celebration. An old stage-coach that will be in the parade is being painted and fixed up right here in Lakeport. Would you like to see it?"

"Oh, yes!" Flossie said. "Can you take us?"

"I'm afraid not," Mr. Dickson said. "I must get back to my shop. But it wouldn't be hard for you to find—that is, if you take your big brother and sister with you."

"Where is the stage-coach?" Freddie asked him.

"Over at Dave Mills' repair and paint shop on

Wells Street," the chemist replied. "It's on the other side of the town."

"Let's go home and get Bert and Nan to go with us, Freddie," Flossie proposed.

"Tell Dave I sent you," the chemist suggested.

The children said good-bye to Mr. Dickson and skipped off.

"Maybe we can play George and Martha Washington in the old coach," Flossie said.

"I'll be the General," Freddie answered.

When they reached home and told Nan and Bert, the older twins were eager to see the old stage-coach. As it was a rather long trip across the town they decided to go on their bicycles.

Freddie and Flossie could not pedal as fast as the bigger children, so Bert and Nan held back a little. Finally they all arrived at Dave Mills' repair and paint shop. Bert introduced the Bobbseys to the good-natured proprietor and said that Mr. Dickson had suggested their coming.

"I'll be glad to show you the coach," Dave Mills said. "It's all painted and fixed up, ready to be delivered."

He led the way into a large back room. In one corner stood the gaily decorated old-time vehicle.

"Oh, it's just like the one Cinderella rode in," Flossie called out, clapping her hands.

Dave Mills laughed. "Well, I hope it won't turn into a pumpkin at midnight," he said. "There are plenty of mice around here at times, and they might try to run off with it."

The twins giggled. Then Dave Mills became serious. He said that the stage-coach had travelled many miles since being built, but that for the past fifty years it had stood in Bartley.

"It's only used when they have a parade," he said. "The last one was twenty-five years ago. Would you children like to hop inside and pretend you're riding?"

Nan and Flossie at once said they would, but Bert and Freddie eyed the driver's high front seat. Noticing this, Dave Mills said they might climb up there.

"You see that box to put your feet on?" he asked.

The boys looked up and saw a large black wooden box directly in front of the driver's seat. Dave explained that this was where valuables were carried in the olden days.

"It's called the boot," he said, then left them as his telephone was ringing.

"Come on, Freddie," Bert urged. "Let's climb up there."

Freddie was not able to do this alone, so Bert went up first and helped his brother. The two boys sat down, Bert in the driver's seat, with Freddie as a guard beside him.

"Are you all ready, ladies?" Bert called out, leaning down.

"Yes, driver," Flossie replied. "Take me to General Washington's home."

"I'm afraid, madam," said Bert, "that Mount Vernon is too far from Lakeport."

"Giddap! Giddap!" cried Freddie, who could not wait for Bert to tell the imaginary horses to move.

The reason Bert had delayed was because he was interested in the boot beneath his legs. He decided to look inside the strong-box. Lifting the lid, he peered inside. There was nothing in the box but a piece of paper, now rather grimy.

Nevertheless, Bert reached down and picked it up. There were words on the paper and, after reading them, he said:

"Say, I've found something pretty good!"

"What is it?" Nan asked, leaning out of the coach window.

"It's a poem," Bert replied. "Listen to this:

> " '*To find my gold*
> *You must be bold.*
> *My Horseshoes and my Fiddle*
> *Are the answer to this riddle!*' "

"That's funny," said Nan. "Read it again."

Bert did, then he added, "Say, this stage-coach came from Bartley. Do you suppose this poem could have anything to do with the money old Mr. Dickson hid?"

"I'll bet it does," said Freddie. "Maybe there's gold in that Horseshoe Lodge!"

CHAPTER VII

A SUDDEN SPILL

"FREDDIE'S right. The gold must be hidden in Horseshoe Lodge!" Bert cried excitedly. "There isn't any other place around where there's a collection of horseshoes."

"Let's ask Dave Mills," Nan suggested.

She hopped out of the stage-coach and ran to the repair shop office. Dave had just finished his telephone conversation and listened in amazement as Nan recited the verse Bert had found in the boot.

"Do you know anything about it?" she asked.

Dave Mills shook his head. "I never looked inside the boot," he said. "This is very strange."

He hurried to the coach with her and read the note himself. He could not even guess what it might mean, he said.

"Many people know about the collection of horseshoes," he went on. "But I never heard of a violin in connection with them."

The twins said they hadn't either, but they would ask Mr. Dickson, the toy-hospital man.

"He's the nephew of the owner of the inn," Nan explained to Dave Mills.

"And a chemist too," said Flossie. "He can glue anything."

Freddie was too excited to wait until they could go over to Mr. Dickson's shop. He asked Nan to telephone him right away.

"That's a good idea," said Dave Mills. "Go in the office and use my phone."

Nan hurried in and dialled the number of the Dickson shop. The chemist answered. When Nan told him about the strange riddle in the note, he said it was just like his uncle to play such a joke. It might well have something to do with the old lodge.

"This makes me begin to think the missing money *might* be hidden there," he said. "But it's still a puzzle."

"Maybe we can find out more when we go to Bartley," Nan offered.

"Let me know," Mr. Dickson said. "But I'm not going to get my hopes up about the money. I'll just work hard at this job."

Nan hung up and returned to the others. She told them what Mr. Dickson had said, and the repair man suggested that Bert put the note back where he had found it.

"Maybe it has something to do with the 175th anniversary," he said, starting back to his office.

"Perhaps they're going to use it at the time of the parade."

The children said nothing, but they were a little disappointed with this explanation. It was much more exciting to think the note had something to do with Horseshoe Lodge.

The idea of hidden gold gave Freddie the inspiration for a new game.

"I want to be a hold-up man and try to take the paper from the boot," he announced. "Come on, let's play cowboys and Indians and robbers!"

Flossie thought this would be fun, too. She was getting a little tired of being a sedate lady riding in the stage-coach. She wanted to be a pioneer woman crossing the Western plains in olden times.

Freddie climbed down and hid himself behind a carton in the repair shop. "All ready!" he shouted.

Bert pretended to urge his six horses forward. As they came around a make-believe bend in the road, Freddie jumped from behind the carton and cried out:

"Stop!"

Bert paid no attention, whipping his horses to make them go fast enough to escape the bandit. But Freddie was insistent.

"Stop!" he shouted loudly.

With this, he climbed up on the front wheel and pulled himself to the seat where Bert was sitting. He tried to open the boot and steal the note. Bert playfully held him so that he could not do it.

Inside the coach Flossie was shrieking as she was sure the ladies in olden times would have done if someone had held up a stage-coach. Nan was laughing so hard that she forgot she too was playing a part.

Suddenly the coach began to sway from side to side. The girls assumed it was because of the tussle which Bert and Freddie were having on the front seat.

A moment later the vehicle lurched violently and a second afterwards it tipped over, hitting the side of the repair shop with a bang. Flossie shrieked in earnest this time.

Bert and Freddie slid across the driver's seat. The older boy managed to hang on, but Freddie toppled to the floor.

"Oh! Oh!" he cried out in pain.

Nan had bumped into Flossie, but recovered her wits in a moment. Opening the upper door of the tilted stage-coach, she climbed out. As she did, she caught a glimpse of two boys running away from the shop.

"They look like Danny Rugg and Jack Westley," she told herself.

Nan would have liked to find out for sure, but she was afraid Freddie was hurt and went at once to help him up from the floor.

"Freddie, did you hurt yourself badly?" she asked quickly.

"I—I banged my arm," he replied.

Nan was thankful that it was no worse. She led Freddie by the hand a little way from the stage-coach and told him to sit on a bench.

By this time Bert had climbed down from the lopsided vehicle, and he helped Nan pull Flossie through the door.

"Are you all right, honey?" Nan asked her little sister.

Flossie was trying not to cry. She had bumped the side of her head and it hurt.

Dave Mills came rushing in and gazed in astonishment. Nan told him she would like to put some ice water on Freddie's and Flossie's bruises.

"I'll get water and towels," Dave said, a look of alarm coming over his face. "There's a wash-basin in my office."

He dashed off, and returned in a moment with two towels dripping with ice water. Nan put one on Flossie's head and told her to hold it there. Then she looked at Freddie's arm.

His elbow was bleeding and the skin just below it was very red. Nan cleaned it off with the ice-cold water, then Dave Mills brought salve and a bandage. While Nan was putting this on Freddie, Dave asked what had happened.

"The stage-coach began to shake all of a sudden," Bert explained. "The next thing I knew it went over."

"I saw two boys running away from here," said

Nan. "I think they came in when we weren't looking and made the coach tip over."

"That was a dreadful thing to do," said Dave Mills angrily. "You children might have been hurt badly."

"I'll try to find out who did it," Bert offered.

Dave Mills asked Bert to help him right the stage-coach. Nan helped too, and presently they were able to push it up so all four wheels stood on the floor.

"The poor coach is all banged up," Flossie said. "Look!"

The side which had hit the wall was marred and smeared. It would need another paint job.

"More bad luck," Flossie sighed.

"Yes, it is bad luck," Dave Mills agreed. "The coach was supposed to go to Bartley this evening. Now it will have to wait over a day or two."

"Perhaps if I help you," Nan offered, "you can get the coach fixed up sooner." She explained that she loved to paint and had had some lessons.

"Well, I'd certainly appreciate your helping me," Dave Mills said. "I'll get some brushes right away."

He went to a corner where cans of paint and tubs of brushes stood. He brought them over and handed a brush to Nan.

"Suppose you fix up that crest design on the door," he suggested. "I'll do the rest."

Nan was very proud to be asked to do this part

of the work. The design was an old Revolutionary family crest and she knew that it would have to be a painstaking job. While she did this and Dave Mills painted the scarred section, the other children played outdoors. Finally, the paint job was finished, and Nan called the twins inside to look at the work.

"The picture looks bee-yoo-ti-ful," Flossie praised her sister.

"Indeed it does," said Dave Mills. "And I think Nan should have a reward, don't you?"

"You mean candy or ice-cream?" Freddie spoke up. He was beginning to realize that it was nearly supper-time.

Dave Mills laughed. "Oh, I mean something better than that," he said. "This stage-coach is going to be hauled to Bartley by six beautiful white horses which are over at Chris's stable. How would you children like to ride to the 175th anniversary celebration in it?"

CHAPTER VIII

A TRICKY GAME

THE Bobbsey twins had a chance to take a long ride in an old-fashioned stage-coach pulled by six white horses!

"Isn't it wonderful?" Nan exclaimed, as the children hurried home to ask their parents' permission to make the trip.

"Do you suppose Dave meant I could drive it?" Bert wondered excitedly.

"I don't know whether I shall be Cinderella or Mrs. Washington," Flossie said importantly.

The minute they reached home, the twins dashed to find their mother. She was in the living-room playing the piano. And Daddy was there too, singing a new song. He had just brought home the sheet-music.

"Mother! Daddy!" Flossie cried out. "We're going to be revolutionary!"

Mrs. Bobbsey took her hands off the keys and Mr. Bobbsey stopped singing.

"What in the world do you mean?" they asked, bursting into laughter.

Bert told of the invitation to ride in the stage-coach all the way to Bartley.

"Well, that is exciting," Mr. Bobbsey said. "I suppose it would be all right. What do you think, Mary?"

The twins' mother agreed. She and Mr. Bobbsey could follow in the family car, she said, just to be sure everything was all right.

"Let's tell Dinah and Sam," Freddie suggested, running towards the kitchen.

When the kindly couple heard the story, they both chuckled. Sam said at once that he ought to go along and be the footman. All ladies and gentlemen who rode in coaches had a footman to help them in and out.

"Oh, yes," Flossie giggled. "And there's a nice seat for you, Sam. It's in the back and up high. You wouldn't mind riding up high, would you?"

Sam said he would not mind this in the least. If Mr. Bobbsey would let him take a little time off from work, he would like very much to go. He said he had a friend living in Bartley and could visit him for a day or two.

"I'll go and ask Daddy right away," Flossie offered, and soon came running back with her father's permission.

"Dinah, why don't you come, too?" the little girl suggested.

Dinah laughed. "Now, honey child, if I went, who would take care of Snap and Waggo and Snoop and give them their food?" she asked.

Snoop was the twins' cat. She kept to herself a good deal because Waggo teased her and she did not like this.

"Well, I guess that's right," Flossie admitted.

The family had supper, then Bert said he would like to go over to Charlie Mason's for a while. He wanted to tell him about the trip.

"All right," Mrs. Bobbsey said. "But be home by nine o'clock, please."

Bert promised and went off. On the way to Charlie's he met the young policeman who had come to Danny Rugg's house. Bert stopped him and asked if the police had found the person who had frightened Chris Ridgeway's horses in the woods.

"No, we haven't," the officer said. "It's very puzzling. I felt sure that Danny Rugg either was responsible or knew something about it. But he denied it."

He told Bert the police felt that whoever the person was, he had been frightened off, because no more explosions had occurred. A detective had been posted in the woods during the middle of the day when most of the riding was done. But he had seen no one.

"Personally I think the prankster will be back," the officer said. "And I'd certainly like to find out who he is."

"I hope you catch him soon," Bert said.

As Bert walked on towards Charlie's, he began to think about how he might help to capture the prankster. He still thought it was Danny. Suddenly Bert snapped his fingers. He might have the answer!

Upon reaching Charlie's house, he said to him, "Would you like to help me catch a person who's playing some mean tricks?"

"I sure would," Charlie replied, grinning. "Are you after Danny Rugg again?"

"How did you guess?" Bert laughed. "Listen, Charlie, I have a plan. The police still haven't caught the person who scared Chris Ridgeway's horses. Now, do you remember I told you about my pony losing a shoe in the woods? When I went back to get it, the shoe was gone. I think the person who caused the noise took the shoe. If I could find out——"

"I get it," said Charlie. "You're going to find out if Danny has the horseshoe. But if he does have one, how will you know if it's the right one?"

"Chris told me Prince's shoe has a star on it," said Bert. "This is what I want to do. Phil Moore lives across the street from Danny. Let's play a game of horseshoes with him. Danny's sure to come over and want to play. If he does, I'll ask him to bring his own horseshoe."

"You're a good detective," Charlie chuckled.

"Let's go first thing tomorrow morning. I have a horseshoe. Have you any?"

"I can borrow one from Sam," Bert replied.

Directly after breakfast Wednesday morning Bert went to Charlie's house. Then the two boys walked over to Phil's. He was a new boy in town and as yet had not met many of the fellows. He was glad to have a game of horseshoes.

"Do you mind if we play on your side lawn?" Bert asked. He wanted to be sure Danny would see them.

"That's okay," said Phil. "I have a horseshoe, too. I'll get it."

The game started and the boys were busy trying their skill when Danny Rugg walked out of his house. He came across the street and stood watching without even saying hello. As Bert finished his turn, he looked up and said:

"Hi, Danny! How's tricks?"

Danny muttered some kind of greeting but said no more. In a few minutes Bert asked him if he would like to join the game.

"Oh, I don't know," Danny said. "You fellows aren't much good. I'd beat you too easy."

"You've got to show me!" Charlie Mason spoke up, nettled. "Have you any horseshoes?"

Danny hesitated a moment, then said yes, he had one. He would get it. As he ran across the street, Bert and Charlie looked at each other, big grins on their faces.

"Let's play partners," Phil Moore suggested. "Who wants to take Danny?"

Phil did not like Danny Rugg any more than Bert and Charlie did, having already had two or three brushes with him since he had moved to Lakeport.

"I'll take Danny," Bert said eagerly.

In this way he would be standing in the pit opposite Danny. Without the other boy becoming suspicious, Bert could see if there were a star on the horseshoe when he picked it up from the pit.

Danny returned and the game started. He won the toss and took his stance. First he pitched Phil's horseshoe and got a ringer, scoring three points.

"That's swell!" Bert shouted encouragingly.

Danny now threw his own horseshoe, which landed close to the first one. He puffed out his chest and strutted around.

"What did I tell you?" he asked.

Charlie pitched next and tried to knock the ringer off, but his shoe did not come close to the stake.

"That puts us ahead, Danny," Bert called, as he leaned down to pick up the horseshoes his partner had thrown.

"Just as I thought!" Bert Bobbsey told himself, staring at the one Danny had brought.

On it was imprinted a star!

Bert almost accused Danny right away of being the one who had caused all the trouble in the woods. But a moment later Bert realized that this would not prove anything. Danny would only deny it all. It would be far better for Bert to catch him in the act of throwing more bombs to scare Chris Ridgeway's horses.

"I'll wait," Bert decided.

When the game, which he and Danny won, was over, Bert suggested to Charlie that they watch Danny's house and trail him when he left it.

"I'm sure he'll go back to the woods soon and play some more tricks," Bert said.

"You're right," Charlie agreed. He too was all for following Danny.

The two boys said good-bye to the others and pretended to go towards their own homes. But they merely circled the block and hid behind a tall hedge to watch Danny's house.

Presently they saw him come out of the front door and walk down the street. When he was a safe distance ahead, Bert and Charlie came from their hiding place and followed him. Two blocks farther on, Danny stopped in front of a house and whistled.

"He's calling Jack Westley," Bert said to Charlie.

Danny and Jack were friends, and between them the two boys played a good many mean tricks on other children. In a moment Jack came outside and the two walked off.

Bert and Charlie kept on their trail. The boys zigzagged through the streets of Lakeport, then set off towards the country. In a little while they came to the wood behind Chris Ridgeway's stables and entered it.

"We mustn't lose the boys," Bert said as he and Charlie followed.

It was hard for them to keep track of Danny and Jack without giving themselves away. The two boys ahead walked stealthily among the trees and bushes, not staying on the trail.

"Look! They're climbing a tree!" Bert whispered presently.

"And here come some riders!" said Charlie. "Now for the fireworks!"

CHAPTER IX

A GIVEAWAY

THE fireworks started in a few moments. As two young women riders came along the trail, a toy bomb hurtled from the tree in which Danny and Jack were hidden. It exploded with a loud bang, and both horses reared.

One of the girls screamed as her horse started galloping ahead wildly. Bert and Charlie ran on to the trail a little distance in front and waved their arms violently. The horse stopped.

"Oh, thank you, boys!" the rider gasped. "Whatever made that dreadful noise?"

"Something dropped from a tree over there," Charlie said.

"It sounded like a bomb," the girl said as her friend came up.

"How frightful!" the other exclaimed.

At this moment they heard quick footsteps and a man appeared along the trail.

"Did you boys make that noise?" he cried, rushing up to the group.

Bert and Charlie shook their heads. Since the man looked as if he did not believe them, the girl on the runaway horse spoke up.

"I'm Susan Smith," she said. "These boys had nothing to do with it. When my horse started to race off, they dashed out and stopped him."

"Good work!" the man said. "I'm a police detective and I have been assigned to this case. Somebody caused the explosion. Did any of you see who did it?"

Bert and Charlie looked at each other. They did not wish to be "squealers".

Susan Smith answered for them. "I think someone up in a tree hurled the bomb," she said.

The detective started a search, but Danny and Jack were well screened by the heavy foliage. The man walked right past the tree in which they were hiding, but he called out:

"You'd better come down! I'll find you sooner or later. If you own up, it'll go easier with you."

Bert and Charlie waited. Danny and Jack did not stir.

"Are we going to let those guys get away with this?" Charlie whispered to Bert.

Bert was about to answer, when suddenly from the tree dropped two more bombs.

CRASH! BANG! *The culprits had given themselves away!*

The detective rushed back and looked up. Still he could not see the hidden boys. But he shouted:

"Do I have to come after you? Or will you come down?"

For a couple of seconds there was not a sound, and then Danny's voice reached their ears. "I'll come down, but I didn't have anything to do with what happened. It's Jack's fault."

"Never mind whose fault it was," the detective said. "You come down here and make it quick!"

The two boys slid down the tree trunk and faced the man. Jack was snivelling, but Danny stood there defiantly.

"We were only having some fun," he said. "You can't prove we frightened anybody."

"You frightened me and my horse," Susan Smith said angrily.

"Your horse scares too easy," Danny said rudely.

"That's enough from you, young man," the detective said. "You boys come along with me."

Danny glared at Bert Bobbsey. "This is all your fault. Why'd you have to follow me?"

The detective turned to Bert and asked what Danny meant. Bert told him the story about the horseshoe with the star on it and the man laughed loudly.

"We ought to put you on the police force," he said. "The real credit for catching these two young rowdies belongs to you."

"I'll get even with you for this!" Danny cried, glowering at Bert.

"If you try it," the detective said, "you'll find yourself in trouble for the second time."

This remark frightened Danny, and he and Jack went off without another word. Susan Smith thanked the boys again, then she and her friend rode away on their horses.

"Charlie," said Bert, "would you like to see the six white horses that are going to pull the stage-coach?"

"I sure would."

Bert led the way to Chris Ridgeway's stable. The riding master was there, just getting ready to take the horses over to Dave Mills' shop and hook up the stage-coach.

"We want to be sure everything is in order before we make the trip," he said. "You Bobbseys are going with us, aren't you?" he asked Bert.

"Yes, we'll be ready right after lunch."

Charlie patted each of the horses in turn. He remarked that he certainly would like to own one of them. Their white coats glistened and their manes had been combed to a silky gloss.

"They're beauties, all right," Charlie said.

"How would you boys like to ride two of them over to Dave Mills'?" Chris asked them.

"You mean it?" Charlie asked excitedly.

Chris saddled horses for the boys and said, "Climb up!"

Bert and Charlie swung themselves into the saddles. Chris said he would ride another and lead the other three in a string behind him.

"I wish I could ride this horse all the way to Bartley," Bert said as they jogged along.

Chris laughed. "I'm afraid you'd be so stiff you wouldn't enjoy the anniversary celebration when you got there," he said.

When they reached the repair shop, the boys helped Dave Mills move the stage-coach out into the open.

"This is really old, isn't it?" Charlie remarked.

He climbed to the driver's seat and Bert hopped up beside him.

"Would you like to see the note in the boot?" Bert asked him.

"You mean the one with the riddle on it?" Charlie asked him. "Sure I would."

Bert lifted the lid and looked inside. To his amazement the strong-box was empty!

"Somebody's taken the note!" he called out.

"What?" Dave Mills asked in surprise. "Someone must have sneaked into my shop and taken it!"

"I'll bet it was Danny Rugg," Bert said. "You remember those two boys Nan said she saw running away from here? She thought one of them was Danny."

"Let's find out," Charlie urged.

But Bert decided that Danny was in enough trouble for the moment. They had better wait until later to talk to him. Anyway, Bert could remember very distinctly what the note said, and repeated it to Charlie:

> "*To find my gold*
> *You must be bold.*
> *My Horseshoes and my Fiddle*
> *Are the answer to this riddle!*"

"That's really a funny one," Charlie remarked. "Have you any idea what the riddle means?"

"No, I haven't," Bert replied. "But when I get to Bartley, I'm certainly going to try to find out."

Directly after luncheon, the Bobbseys gathered in the living-room, ready for their trip. Dinah was helping the younger ones with their coats. Freddie had collected all the baggage in the front hall and said he wanted to pile it on top of the stage-coach.

"I'm afraid that wouldn't be wise," his mother said. "The stage-coach is very old. Suppose you pick out one small bag for the top."

"I'll take Flossie's," Freddie said.

The bag was a colourful plaid one and would look very well on top as they rode along, the little boy thought.

"Is everyone ready?" Mr. Bobbsey called out, coming down the stairs.

"Yes," said Nan. "And I have the bottle of glue dissolvent from Mr. Dickson."

In a few moments the family heard the clatter of

horses' hooves around the corner. The stage-coach was arriving!

"Well now, that sure is a fine sight!" exclaimed Dinah, stepping to the front porch and watching as Chris drove up and brought the horses to a halt.

The children dashed from the house to look at it. Neighbours and playmates came hurrying from their homes to see the unusual vehicle.

"Where's Sam?" Mrs. Bobbsey asked, as they were ready to climb in.

"Right here, Mrs. Bobbsey."

When Sam walked out of the front door of the house, everyone gasped. Sam wore red knee breeches, a white satin coat, and his grey curly hair was covered with a three-cornered black hat.

"Sam!" cried Flossie, rushing up to him. "Sam, you look just bee-yoo-ti-ful!"

Sam grinned, then bowed with great dignity and said:

"Now I can properly help all my folks in and out of the coach."

First he assisted Nan to step up. Next he helped Flossie, and finally Freddie. Then he closed the door. Bert waited for Sam to help him up to the seat beside Chris Ridgeway.

When everyone was in place, Sam climbed up to the little seat high behind the coach. He folded his arms and looked straight ahead.

The Bobbseys were off for the anniversary celebration!

CHAPTER X

A BUMPY TRIP

"GOOD-BYE, Nan!" called Nellie Parks.

"Good-bye, Bert!" Charlie Mason shouted.

Flossie's friend, Susie Larker, and Freddie's special little playmate, Teddy Blake, were there too. They waved gaily as the stage-coach started off for Bartley with the Bobbsey twins.

Dinah waved to them also. She was holding Waggo by the collar because she knew that the minute she let him go, he would want to run after the coach. The dog yipped frantically, but she would not release him.

"So long, everybody!" Bert called out from his seat beside Chris Ridgeway.

Nan, Flossie and Freddie leaned from the stage-coach window and called good-bye. Sam grinned happily from his high perch. Then Chris said:

"Tch! Tch!"

The six beautiful white horses started off. Mr. and Mrs. Bobbsey stepped into their car and slowly followed. As the procession reached the main street of Lakeport, people smiled and waved.

"What an unusual sight!" said one woman on a street corner, and began to clap. "I wonder where they're heading."

"I think to the 175th anniversary at Bartley," replied a newspaper photographer standing next to her. He worked on the local paper and was busy taking pictures of the Bobbseys.

"Well, if the whole celebration's as interesting as that stage-coach," the woman said, "I believe I'll go up to Bartley and see it."

Shopkeepers and customers hurried outside to find out what the excitement was about. The children kept waving as did Sam and Chris Ridgeway. Suddenly Bert called down to Nan:

"Look who's coming!"

Riding quickly up the street on bicycles were Danny Rugg and Jack Westley. In a moment they had caught up to the stage-coach.

"Who said you could ride in that?" Danny asked the twins.

The Bobbseys did not reply. They were too busy smiling and calling to various people they knew along the sidewalk. When Danny asked the same question for the third time, Flossie became annoyed. She leaned out of the window and called up to Sam as a Colonial lady might have:

"Clear the road of these nuisances!"

The bystanders laughed. Danny and Jack did

not move, though Sam asked them to. Finally Freddie called out:

"You'd better leave. You almost ruined this stage-coach once by knocking it over in the repair shop."

"Aw, I didn't hurt it," Danny answered without thinking. Then suddenly he realized he had said too much. He and Jack dashed down a side street on their bicycles.

"Good for you, Freddie," Bert called down. "You found out just what we wanted to know."

Flossie sighed. "It would just be our bad luck to have Danny show up in Bartley," she said. "Why does that old meanie always have to get in our way?"

By this time the stage-coach had reached the end of the business section and now turned into the highway which led to Bartley. For some time the horses trotted at a good pace. But as an uphill grade began, they slowed down.

"This ride is getting bumpy," Flossie said presently. "How far is it to Bartley?" she called out of the window to Chris Ridgeway.

He said it was a good many miles. If the children were uncomfortable, perhaps they ought to transfer to the Bobbsey car.

"Oh, that wouldn't be any fun at all," Freddie objected, and Flossie said no more.

They rode along for a while, then at a turn in the road, came a big detour sign. The main highway was being repaired, so the coach was forced to take a side road which was very rutty. Nan and the small twins found the riding hard to take.

"I suppose ladies in older times didn't complain," said Flossie as she jounced around. "But I'm glad we d-don't have to take such b-bumpy rides nowadays."

Freddie decided it would be better to stand up. He found it much more comfortable than sitting on the wooden seat with its thin cushion. But he swayed from side to side and had to hold on to a strap.

Presently the stage-coach started up a very steep hill. The horses walked very slowly. Freddie poked his head out of the window to look around.

"It's nice in the country," he said. "I can see a farm with a lot of cows."

Flossie stood up and looked also. But Nan did not think it was safe for them to be so near the door while the stage-coach was moving, and asked them to sit down.

Freddie and Flossie did so for a few moments, then Freddie was up again. He had just started to lean out of the window when the coach rolled over a high bump in the road, jolting them all severely. The next instant the door flew open and Freddie fell out!

"Oh!" Nan cried and yelled to the horses, "Whoa! Stop!"

Chris Ridgeway pulled them to a halt and Nan jumped out. To her relief Freddie was getting up and did not seem to be hurt.

"Are you all right?" she asked, brushing him off.

"I—I guess so," he answered.

Flossie had hopped out of the coach, too. "I'm glad this wasn't a concrete road," she said.

From a little distance behind them Mr. and Mrs. Bobbsey had seen the accident. Mr. Bobbsey drove ahead quickly and he and his wife jumped from the car.

"Freddie! Freddie! Are you hurt?" Mrs. Bobbsey cried.

"No, Mummy. Really I'm not," the little boy insisted. "I guess I bounced."

Nevertheless, Mrs. Bobbsey thought that Nan and the young twins had had enough of the stage-coach riding for this trip. She insisted that they come into the car with her and Mr. Bobbsey.

"I believe we'll go ahead," she told Bert, Chris and Sam. "It'll be rather late when we get to Bartley and I think we should find rooms. What time will you arrive, Chris?"

"About seven o'clock, I should say," he replied.

"Suppose I meet you in front of the old lodge," Mr. Bobbsey suggested.

After saying good-bye to Bert, the rest of the Bobbseys stepped into the car and rode off. On the outskirts of Bartley they saw an attractive hotel. Mr. Bobbsey parked and asked for rooms.

"I'm sorry," said the proprietor, "but nothing is left."

The twins' father went on into town and stopped at an inn. The answer here was the same: no rooms left. After this Mr. Bobbsey stopped at every guest house in the main section of Bartley. Each place was filled with visitors.

"Goodness, what are we going to do?" Mrs. Bobbsey asked. "I had no idea there would be so many people in town."

"We'll go through every street and see if we can find anything," her husband replied.

On a side road, down which they turned because there was a sign advertising rooms for rent, they came upon the old Bartley Lodge.

"Oh," cried Nan, "isn't it wonderful!"

"But spooky looking, all shut up," said Flossie.

The stone structure was two stories high and had several massive chimneys. All the shutters were closed and the front door was boarded up.

"What a shame!" said Mrs. Bobbsey. "There is real grandeur to that old building. It's too bad it had to be condemned."

As they passed the long structure, they saw the wooden wing at one end where old Mr. Dickson had lived and where there now was a caretaker.

"Which part do you suppose the gold's hidden in?" Freddie asked suddenly.

"Well, if I had to guess," his father laughed,

"I'd say one of those big chimneys would be a fine hiding place."

"It might be in the cellar," Nan suggested.

"Or under that stable over there," Freddie said, pointing to another large building at the rear.

Mr. Bobbsey drove on. Not far beyond was the house that had rooms for rent. He went inside to inquire of the woman who owned the place, but was told that everything had been rented for some time.

"I'm sure you won't find any rooms in town," she told him. "We've never had so many visitors."

Mr. Bobbsey returned to the car and reported the sad news. He said he guessed they would have to turn around and go back to Lakeport.

"Dad," said Nan, "I have an idea. Why don't we go to Joy Lambert's house and ask her? She's Nellie Parks' cousin, you remember." Nan took a paper from her pocket-book and handed it to her father. The address was on it.

Mrs. Bobbsey thought this was a good plan, so Mr. Bobbsey turned the car around and went in the direction of the Lambert home.

When they reached it, Nan got out and rang the door-bell. Joy came to the door.

"Nan Bobbsey!" she shrieked in delight. "Where did you come from?"

"Hi, Joy!" Nan said. "We can't find a place to sleep. My family are out in the car. Could you tell us any place to go?"

"I'll ask my dad and mother," Joy said. "Won't you all come in?"

Nan called to her family, but Mr. Bobbsey said they would wait in the car for her. She stepped into the house and followed Joy to the living-room.

"Our bedrooms are crammed with relatives," Joy whispered laughingly. "Otherwise, you all could stay here."

She introduced Nan to her father and mother, an aunt and uncle, two cousins, and her grandmother. Nan acknowledged their greetings and smiled to herself—the Lambert household certainly was full of relatives!

Upon hearing Nan's story, Mrs. Lambert looked disturbed. "I'm afraid there isn't a room to be rented in the town of Bartley," she said. "The 175th celebration is very popular and people who used to live here in former years have come in droves to stay for a few days."

"There's just one place where nobody's staying," Mr. Lambert suggested. "It's possible I could arrange for you Bobbseys to stay there. Suppose I go out and talk to your family about it, Nan."

He went with her to the car and she introduced her parents and the twins.

"I'm certainly sorry to hear about your predicament," Mr. Lambert said. "I'm the building inspector for Bartley, and I might be able to get permission for you to stay in the wing of the old Bartley Lodge."

As the Bobbseys looked at him in amazement, he went on to say that the caretaker lived alone on the first floor. There were three bedrooms on the second floor of the wing which were not used.

"It's perfectly safe to stay in that part of the building," he said. "I'll be glad to find out if it would be all right."

"That's very kind of you," Mrs. Bobbsey said, and Mr. Bobbsey added, "Would you inquire, please?"

Freddie's and Flossie's eyes grew large with excitement. It was possible they were going to stay at Horseshoe Lodge—the place where gold might be hidden; the place with a strange collection of horseshoes; the place that held a mystery no one had solved!

CHAPTER XI

MISSING TWINS

MR. LAMBERT went to telephone. He returned in a few minutes to tell the Bobbseys he had received permission for them to stay in the wing of the old lodge.

"I'll be glad to take you over there and introduce you to Ben Stillman, the caretaker," he said. "Ben's rather a strange fellow—perfectly all right, but he doesn't talk much."

Mr. Lambert got his own car and led the way to Horseshoe Lodge. Joy rode with the Bobbseys and warned them to be careful if they went into the old part of the building.

"I don't mean it's going to fall down and hurt you," she giggled. "I just mean look out for spooks."

Mrs. Bobbsey laughed, then said, "Joy, are you trying to scare my children?"

"Oh, spooks and ghosts are fun," Joy said. "I hope you meet lots of them."

Nan laughed, but Freddie and Flossie were very serious about the whole thing. They wondered if strange things might happen while they were playing in the closed-up part of the lodge.

Mr. Bobbsey and Mr. Lambert stopped their cars in front of the old hotel and they all walked up the path to the wing. Ben Stillman let them in and Mr. Lambert explained that he had received permission for these friends of his to have rooms.

Ben, a tall gaunt man with grey hair, did not speak; merely nodded. Mr. Lambert introduced each of the Bobbseys in turn, and again the caretaker acknowledged the introduction by bobbing his head.

"Would you like us to wait while you get the rooms ready?" Mrs. Bobbsey asked him.

The elderly man shook his head, motioned with his finger for them to follow him and led the way up a narrow stairway. The Lamberts said goodbye.

"I'll be seeing you," Joy called, and Nan answered, "Real soon."

Then she followed the others upstairs. Ben opened the doors to the bedrooms and Mrs. Bobbsey said she and her husband would take the centre one. The two girls would sleep in the room on one side and the boys in the other.

Each room had a big fireplace, with logs laid ready for use. There were attractive curtains at the windows and each room contained a huge old-fashioned bed. The coverlets were pretty, hand-made patchwork quilts.

"My bed is awful high up," Flossie complained. "How am I going to get in it?"

The bed was high indeed, and the top of the mattress was level with the little girl's head.

"They're feather-beds," Ben Stillman explained.

Flossie was glad that he had spoken, because she had begun to wonder whether he was able to speak. He leaned down and from under the bed pulled out a little step-ladder. He pointed to it and Flossie walked up the three steps. She flopped on top of the bed and looked around. "This will be like sleeping in an airplane," she giggled.

A faint smile played over Ben Stillman's face, but he did not say anything. Instead, he turned and walked out of the door and went downstairs noiselessly.

"He's just like a pussy-cat," Flossie stated. "He's so quiet and he doesn't talk."

"If Ben makes no more noise moving about than he does talking," Mr. Bobbsey said, "we'll never know he's in the house."

"And I suggest," Mrs. Bobbsey added, smiling, "that we don't make much noise either, so we won't annoy Ben Stillman."

"How soon can we see the old part of this lodge?" Freddie asked.

His mother said they must go out and get supper. Perhaps it would be best to wait until the next morning, then ask Ben to show them through the hotel.

"I think Bert should be arriving any minute," Mr. Bobbsey stated. "I'll go downstairs and wait for him."

Nan said she would help her mother unpack the suit-cases. While they were busy doing this, the little twins went downstairs. Mrs. Bobbsey, seeing them go, thought that they were planning to watch the arrival of the stage-coach.

But Freddie had other ideas, and whispered to his twin that it would be fun to go down and see what they could find out about the old part of the lodge. Flossie agreed, saying:

"I suppose it won't hurt to take one teeny, tiny peek."

They reached the foot of the stairs and looked at a door which Freddie figured must lead into the hotel. As he put his hand on the knob, there was a noise in the street.

The stage-coach was arriving and Mr. Bobbsey went out to greet the riders. Sam was not with Bert and Chris, and the boy explained that they had left Sam at his friend's house.

"Where are we going to stay in Bartley, Dad?" Bert asked.

"Right here at the lodge," Mr. Bobbsey replied.

Bert's eyes popped. "Really?" he yelled. "That's nifty. Then we'll be right on the spot to hunt for the hidden gold."

Chris Ridgeway laughed. He wished Bert luck and added that he hoped all the Bobbseys would enjoy their stay at the old hotel without seeing too many ghosts. He said good-bye, telling them that after he delivered the stage-coach and horses, a friend would drive him back to Lakeport.

"Thanks a lot for the ride," Bert said.

Chris waved. "If you find the note that belongs in the boot, or locate the hidden gold, let me know!" he called.

Bert promised that he would and went inside the lodge with his father. After the boy had carried Flossie's suit-case to her room, Mr. Bobbsey suggested that they all go downtown and eat supper.

"Where are Freddie and Flossie?" he asked.

"Why, they went downstairs," his wife replied. "I thought they were with you."

"I haven't seen them," the twins' father said. "Maybe Ben knows where they are."

He hurried down the steps, followed by the others. Mr. Bobbsey knocked on Ben Stillman's first-floor apartment, but there was no answer.

"Do you suppose the children went into the old part of the lodge?" Mr. Bobbsey asked, looking at the door which led from the hall of the wing to the condemned part of the hotel.

He opened it and peered in. There was nothing ahead of them but inky blackness.

"Freddie! Flossie!" he called.

There was no answer.

"Where could they be?" Mrs. Bobbsey was becoming worried.

Mr. Bobbsey knocked again on Ben Stillman's door. Still receiving no reply, he turned the knob. The door was not locked, so they walked inside. Lights were burning in the room, but no one was in sight.

"Let's look in the other rooms," Mrs. Bobbsey suggested.

She led the way to the tiny kitchen of Ben's quarters. As they stood in the doorway, suddenly the centre of the floor began to tilt. Everyone waited tensely, fear creeping into their hearts. A trapdoor was rising silently with no one in view.

Nan's heart was pounding furiously. Were they about to be introduced to the ghost of the lodge?

But, a second later, Ben Stillman's head suddenly appeared. In a moment he stepped into the room.

Without saying a word, the man turned and looked into the opening, then held his hand down. Flossie Bobbsey came up a wooden stairway. Freddie followed her.

"What a scare you gave us!" Mrs. Bobbsey cried. "Children, why didn't you tell me where you were going?"

"It's my fault," Ben said, but did not explain why.

Flossie did, though. She said that Ben Stillman grew lots and lots of little white buttons in his cellar and had shown her and Freddie how he did it.

"Mushrooms," Ben corrected.

"He has boxes and boxes of them," Freddie added. "And did you know that mushrooms have little gills to breathe with just like fish do?"

"And they raise them in cellars so they'll keep nice and white," Flossie added.

"Well, I'm glad you children learned so much about mushrooms," Mrs. Bobbsey said, "but please, next time you're planning to disappear, let me know."

She told Ben Stillman that they were going out to supper but would return in a short time. He merely nodded and turned to go back down into his mushroom cellar.

On the way to the restaurant, Flossie told the others that she and Freddie had talked to Ben Stillman about the mystery. They had mentioned the riddle and asked him if he knew what it meant.

"But he never heard of it," Flossie reported.

"I told him about the fiddle and asked him if he plays one," Freddie said.

"What did he say?" Nan asked.

"He said he can't play anything," Flossie replied.

"He's never heard of the buried gold, either. I guess Ben doesn't know anything about the mystery," Freddie concluded.

"No doubt you're right, Freddie," said Mrs. Bobbsey. "Now let's forget the mystery for a while, and look at these exhibits in the windows as we go along."

Every shop in Bartley was decorated for the celebration. Some had displays of old hand-made clothing and furniture. And there were all sorts of old-fashioned toys which children had played with a hundred and seventy-five years before.

"Tomorrow we'll see the whole town," Mrs. Bobbsey promised, smiling.

The children enjoyed their supper, but began to yawn before it was over. As soon as they had eaten, the family went back to the lodge and prepared for bed. The small twins were asleep in a short time and it was not long before Bert and Nan had climbed up into the high feather-beds and were asleep, too.

Nan snuggled down beside her little sister and chuckled. She had sunk so far into the fluffy feather-bed that she could barely see over the side of it.

The next thing Nan knew, she was suddenly awake and wondering where she was. It was very dark and it took her a few seconds to realize she was spending the night in a strange room.

"I wonder what woke me up," she thought.

Then suddenly she knew. Coming clearly to her ears was the sound of a violin being played. At once Nan's thoughts flew to the riddle:

> *My Horseshoes and my Fiddle*
> *Are the answer to this riddle.*

Where was the sound coming from? Nan hopped out of bed and walked to the window. No, the violin playing was not outdoors.

Turning back, she passed the fireplace. Then she realized that the music was coming out of the chimney!

CHAPTER XII

A PICNIC BREAKFAST

TO be certain she was not dreaming, Nan Bobbsey decided to awaken someone else. She looked at Flossie a moment, sleeping peacefully.

"No, I won't disturb her," Nan decided. "I'll get Bert."

She hurried into the hall and went to her brother's room. Bert was so sound asleep it was several seconds before she could awaken him. Upon learning, though, that Nan had heard violin playing, he sat up and listened intently. But there was no sound of music now.

"Are you sure you heard it?" he asked his twin.

"Well, I'm not dreaming, am I?"

"Of course not," Bert replied.

He jumped out of bed and followed Nan into the hall. Still they heard no music. They went into Nan and Flossie's room. Here the sounds of violin playing came distinctly to their ears.

"It seems to be coming out of the chimney," Nan whispered.

Bert lay down on the floor and put his head inside the fireplace. Looking up, he could see the stars shining above, nothing more.

Next the boy put his ear against the floor of the fireplace. Now he could hear the music more plainly.

"It's coming from down below," he said.

Nan dropped to the floor and listened. The piece of music was not familiar to her or Bert. It had a doleful sound and a moment later ended in a minor key.

"Let's go down and ask Ben Stillman about it," Nan whispered.

"Okay," Bert agreed, and the two children tip-toed quietly down the stairs.

They tapped on Ben's door but there was no answer. Bert rapped a little louder, but Nan stopped him when he gave a harder thump.

"Maybe we shouldn't awaken the poor man," she said. "The music has stopped anyway."

"Do you suppose it was he playing?" Bert asked, puzzled. "Say, maybe *he's* the ghost around this place!"

Whispering, the twins discussed this idea. Ben Stillman seemed like the kind of person who did not care to have other people around. It was possible that when visitors came to the lodge, he would try in one way or another to scare them away.

"Maybe he's trying to get rid of us," Bert whispered. "But he can't scare me!"

"I guess we'd better go back to bed," Nan replied. "We'll tell Dad and Mother about it in the morning."

She and Bert had just started up the stairs when they heard a loud cry from the second floor. Fearful, the twins flew up the steps two at a time to see what had happened. Reaching the top, they could hear whimpering in Nan's room.

The twins dashed in and Bert turned on the light. Flossie was sitting up in bed, looking wild-eyed.

"Nan, where did you go?" she wailed. "I woke up and you weren't here and—and I heard funny music."

As Nan hurried over to soothe her little sister, Mr. and Mrs. Bobbsey ran into the room. They asked if Flossie had had a nightmare.

"Maybe that's what you'd call it," Flossie answered. "But if it was, I don't want any more. Mother, music was coming right out of the wall."

Mrs. Bobbsey hastened to the bed and put her arm around her small daughter. She said that this was not possible. Flossie must have had a bad dream. She should try to go to sleep again.

"Flossie didn't imagine it, Mother," Nan said and she told how she had been awakened by the sound of violin playing.

Mr. and Mrs. Bobbsey looked at her in

amazement, but before they had a chance to say anything, a new figure hurried into the room. It was Ben Stillman, wearing a long old-fashioned nightgown and a little cap on his head.

The Bobbseys expected him to say something, but he just stood there, staring at them. Mr. Bobbsey explained what had happened and asked if he could tell them about the music.

Ben Stillman shook his head. Then he said, "At night people are supposed to sleep," and turned and went downstairs.

Bert grinned. "Well, we didn't find out much," he remarked.

"Whatever the strange playing was," Mr. Bobbsey said, "it hasn't harmed any of us. I think we should all go back to bed."

Mrs. Bobbsey waited for a few moments to be sure Flossie was over her fright and that Nan was not nervous. Then she went back to her own room.

The next time the children awakened it was morning and the sun was shining brightly. In a little while Mrs. Bobbsey came in to say that breakfast was ready in her bedroom. The twins' father had risen early and gone downtown to get some food.

"Is it going to be a picnic breakfast?" Flossie asked. Flossie adored picnics.

"I guess you could call it that," her mother replied, smiling. "It's a surprise anyway. Daddy didn't say what he bought."

When the family assembled, Mr. Bobbsey opened a large box which he had set on the bureau. Inside it were eighteen small round cartons. He took out two at a time and handed them around.

"Why, it's a regular breakfast," Flossie said, opening the three cartons which were passed to her.

One contained orange juice, another oatmeal with cream and sugar on it, and a third held milk.

While they were eating, there was a knock on the door. Bert opened it and Ben Stillman stepped inside.

"I am going out," he announced. "Here's a key."

"Oh!" Freddie exclaimed. "I was going to ask you to show us through the lodge."

"Later," the caretaker said. He stepped back, closed the door and went off.

The older Bobbseys were amused by the man's abrupt manner of speech, but the twins were disappointed at his announcement. They had wanted to start their search that very morning.

Mrs. Bobbsey, reading their thoughts, said that first they should do some sightseeing. Since they had come to Bartley to see the 175th anniversary celebration, they ought to tour the town that morning.

"I must beg off," said the twins' father. "I have to go and find out about the plywood—my original reason for coming to Bartley, you remember."

All the family walked downtown together, then Mr. Bobbsey went off by himself. After the twins and their mother had strolled along and looked in the shop windows for about twenty minutes, they came to a museum.

"We certainly should go in here and find out about the history of Bartley," Mrs. Bobbsey remarked.

Freddie held back. He was not particularly interested in museums for grown-ups.

"Do they have anything in there for children?" he asked his mother.

She smiled. "The only way to find out, Freddie, is to go inside."

When they entered, he looked all around at the various glass cases holding old jewellery, books, newspapers and souvenirs.

He could not read any of the writing because it was in old-fashioned script. The little boy soon became bored.

"Let's go to another place," he begged.

"I'll show you something good," Bert offered.

He had noticed a room where a cannon stood in the centre of the floor. He led Freddie to it and showed him how soldiers had put cannon balls into it during the Revolutionary War.

Freddie was interested for a little while, then he was determined to go outside. Finally his mother gave in and all the Bobbseys returned to the sidewalk.

As they walked up one street and down another, Freddie looked for two things—the local fire station and also fire alarms like those on certain street corners in Lakeport. Not seeing any, he asked his mother where they were located.

"I'm sure there's a fire station in town," she said. "But as for the fire alarms, well, I suppose if there's a fire, the people either run to the fire station itself or use their telephones."

As she finished speaking, the little group came in front of an old church. Mrs. Bobbsey said that this was one of the buildings they surely must visit. She turned into the brick walk and mounted the steps. The twins followed, but still Freddie kept wishing that there would be a fire or at least some other kind of excitement.

At one side of the vestibule a long rope hung down from the ceiling. The little boy wondered what it was for. But he had no chance to find out, for his mother took him by the hand and whisked him inside the church.

Freddie looked around dutifully and listened as Mrs. Bobbsey pointed out the beautiful stained glass windows and the fine organ.

Finally the tour was over and they returned to the vestibule. Letting go of his mother's hand, Freddie dashed over to the rope and took hold of it.

"I'm going to climb up," the boy told himself.

He hoisted himself up on the rope and started swinging from side to side.

"What fun!" he thought.

Suddenly a mighty sound shattered the stillness.

The church bells were ringing violently. The harder Freddie swung, the louder they rang.

BONG! BONG! BONG!

"Freddie, get down!" Mrs. Bobbsey exclaimed, rushing over to him.

Freddie was enjoying his ride. But after one more swing, he slid down the rope and dropped to the floor. The bells jangled for several moments, then the sound died away.

As it did, other sounds filled the air. A fire engine siren began to scream. A police car raced up the street, its own siren wailing frantically.

On the sidewalk, people began running from various buildings towards the church. The Bobbsey twins and their mother stared in utter astonishment.

"Oh, what has happened?" Nan cried out.

CHAPTER XIII

A SPOOKY TOUR

AS the twins stood on the church steps with their mother, people rushed up to them excitedly. They all wanted to know what was the matter.

"I don't understand," said Mrs. Bobbsey.

"Was the bank robbed?" a man called across the crowd.

"Was there an accident on the river?" a woman cried.

Still another asked if there had been a factory explosion. The Bobbseys stood speechless. At this moment Ben Stillman pushed his way through the crowd and ran up to them.

"Who rang the church bells?" he demanded.

"I—I did," Freddie said.

"What!" the caretaker cried out. "You bad boy! You're responsible for all this!"

"Me?" Freddie asked, dumbfounded. "How?"

Before Ben Stillman could explain, two firemen

ran up the church steps from one side and several policemen from the other.

"Where's the trouble?" one of the officers asked.

"I guess there's no trouble," said Mrs. Bobbsey, "except that my small son, quite by accident, rang your church bells. We arrived in Bartley only last night and he never dreamed that the ringing of the church bells would bring all of you here. Would you mind telling me the reason for it?"

"In this town," one of the policemen said, "we only ring church bells on Sunday except in an emergency. If there is a big accident involving several people, someone rings these bells and the whole town turns out to help."

"I see," said Mrs. Bobbsey. "Well, we're dreadfully sorry that we caused this trouble. My son saw the bell-rope dangling in the vestibule and pulled it. We had no idea it would upset all of Bartley."

Freddie was shaking with fright. He had only intended having a little fun because he was bored with sightseeing. Now the townspeople and visitors in Bartley were all staring at him. Those who had not yet heard what had happened were still awaiting orders to go and help in some great emergency.

Another policeman walked to the top step of the church and in a loud voice told the crowd what had happened. As they walked off some mumbled angrily, but most of the people merely shook their heads smiling, as if to say:

"What will children do next?"

"Where's the sexton?" the policeman asked the Bobbseys.

"We didn't see anyone around," Bert said.

The officer called out the name of Silas, but the sexton did not answer.

"Probably he went home," the policeman said. "Well, he never should have left the bell-rope hanging this way so that small boys could get hold of it."

At this moment the fire chief walked into the vestibule and eyed the dangling rope. Then, going part way up a circular stairway which led to the balcony, he reached far over and grabbed the rope. He tied it around a hook high in the wall. As he descended the stairs, he noticed the woebegone look on Freddie's face. Going up to him, the chief said:

"It's all right, little fellow. Accidents are sometimes the result of just trying to have fun. No damage was done, so forget the whole thing and have a good time."

Freddie brightened immediately. He liked the fire chief and told him that when he grew up he wanted to be a fireman himself.

"You don't suppose," the little boy half whispered, "you don't suppose I could have a ride on your fire engine?"

The captain looked down at Freddie and smiled. "Well, I don't see any reason why not," he said, "especially since you want to be a fireman when you grow up. Come along."

Freddie was thrilled. He forgot all about the trouble he had caused and proudly climbed up on the engine. He waved to his family and said he would meet them at the fire station.

Flossie sighed. "Freddie's an in-and-out-of-trouble man, isn't he?" she said, and the others laughed.

After they had picked Freddie up, speechless with joy after his ride on the engine, they all went back to the old lodge. Ben Stillman had returned and Bert asked him if it would be possible to look through the old part.

"I'll get a light," the caretaker said by way of consent.

After obtaining a flashlight, he opened the door to the gloomy corridor leading into the unused part of the old hotel. It was cool and musty smelling in the building, and the floor creaked. Flossie kept tight hold of her sister's hand.

There were several doors along the way, but each one was closed. Nan told Ben Stillman she had heard they were tightly glued. The man made no comment.

Presently they came into the main lobby and the caretaker flashed his light around the wall. On one side was the clerk's desk with the large register still on it. The book lay open and the children glanced at the signatures. The last person who had signed his name in the book was Chris Ridgeway, Lakeport.

"Why, we know him!" Flossie told Ben. "He brought us here in the stage-coach."

The caretaker smiled, but did not speak. He beamed the light on the great oak front door. It was massive and elaborately carved.

"It's sad to think nobody's ever going to come through that door again and stay at this hotel," Nan remarked.

"Yes, it is." Flossie wagged her head dolefully.

"Where are the horseshoes?" Bert asked the caretaker.

Ben flashed his light on the rear wall of the lobby. The twins and Mrs. Bobbsey could hardly believe their eyes. Hundreds of horseshoes hung there in rows. How many different sizes there were —from very large to very small! The Bobbseys walked over to look at them.

"This shoe was worn by Paul Revere's horse," Ben Stillman said, pointing to one in the centre of the collection.

"It must be very valuable," Mrs. Bobbsey exclaimed.

Ben Stillman merely shrugged. He read out several other names written above the horseshoes: "George Washington, Buffalo Bill, Man o' War."

"Who are Buffalo Bill and Man o' War?" Freddie asked.

When the caretaker did not reply, Mrs. Bobbsey

told the children that Buffalo Bill's right name was William Cody. He lived at the time of the Civil War and was one of the riders in the Pony Express mail service from Missouri to California.

"Later, when a railroad was being built from Kansas to the Pacific Coast," she said, "Cody supplied the workmen with buffalo meat. That's how he got his nickname."

"Didn't he have something to do with a circus too?" Bert asked.

"Yes, he did," Mrs. Bobbsey replied. "Buffalo Bill founded his great Wild West Show and toured the United States and Europe with it."

"Was the Wild West Show like a rodeo?" Nan asked.

"Yes, it was."

"And who was Man o' War?" Freddie inquired again.

"A great racehorse," Mrs. Bobbsey said.

Suddenly Ben Stillman pointed to one of the shoes in the third row of the collection. He muttered something and then said, "There was a sapphire in this horseshoe. It's gone!"

"You mean it fell out?" Bert asked.

The caretaker shook his head. "It was in here only a few days ago. It must have been stolen!"

They all looked at one another. Someone had sneaked into Horseshoe Lodge and taken the valuable sapphire!

"I'm surprised," the twins' mother remarked,

"that after the lodge was closed up such a valuable horseshoe would be left here."

"Old Mr. Dickson didn't want a thing touched," the caretaker explained. "This horseshoe originally belonged to a friend of his who put sapphires in all his pet horses' shoes. Well," he said abruptly, "we'd better go now. I'll have to report this to the police."

The Bobbseys had barely left the lobby when there was a loud thump behind them. They all turned to look and the caretaker flashed his light around. The horseshoe from which the sapphire was missing had fallen to the floor.

"Oo-ee!" Flossie squealed. "It's more bad luck for us! See, the horseshoe has its back turned towards us!"

CHAPTER XIV

FREDDIE'S FROG

THE caretaker of Horseshoe Lodge looked at Flossie and said, "Maybe it is bad luck."

"If a ghost lives in this lodge," Freddie said, "maybe he knocked down the horseshoe."

Ben Stillman looked at the little boy severely. "Haven't your parents told you there aren't any such things as ghosts?" he demanded.

With this, the caretaker started walking back along the hallway to his own quarters. The Bobbseys followed.

The twins would have liked to stay longer and investigate more of the old building, but without a light they could not do this. Bert determined that he would go downtown soon and buy a couple of flashlights.

"Mother," Nan said as they reached the wing of the old hotel, "do you think it would be all right to try Mr. Dickson's glue dissolvent on one of the doors?"

"Not without permission," her mother replied. "Mr. Stillman, do you know who has charge of this lodge?"

"The bank," was the caretaker's brief reply.

Mrs. Bobbsey had a hard time finding out from him which bank it was and which man she should see to speak to about the lodge. But finally she learned that it was a Mr. Hall at the Bartley Trust Company.

"Suppose we all walk down there and see him," she suggested. "Then we'll have lunch."

As they were about to leave the house, Sam came up the street. He said good morning and asked if his "folks" were having a nice time.

"Oh, yes," said Flossie. "Only we had a big scare last night."

She told Sam about the mysterious violin music, and he chuckled. He said that if they needed any help, they should get in touch with him—he would come running and catch any ghosts that were after the twins.

"We'll remember," Flossie promised.

"Mrs. Bobbsey," Sam said, "is Mr. Bobbsey here?"

When he learned that his employer had gone off to see about some plywood, Sam said he had stopped by to ask if he might stay in Bartley a few days.

"We're not busy right now back at the lumber-yard," he explained, "and my friend Rufus the blacksmith has so many horses to get ready for the parade, he doesn't see how he'll ever get through. He wants me to help him."

"I'm sure it will be all right, Sam," Mrs. Bobbsey told him. "But I'll let you know definitely when Mr. Bobbsey returns this evening."

"Then I'll go back to Rufus's and wait," Sam said. Turning to the boys, he added, "I believe you'd like it over at Rufus's shop. Have you ever seen a horse shod?"

"I never have," said Freddie.

Bert had once been to a blacksmith's, but he said that right now he would rather watch Rufus and Sam at work than go to the bank.

"All right," his mother agreed. "But meet us in time for lunch at the Robin's Egg Restaurant."

"Why does a horse have to wear shoes, anyway?" Freddie asked Sam, hurrying to keep pace with him.

"Well," Sam began, "it's like this. A wild horse never goes on hard roads or hard ground. And he never pulls anything heavy, or carries a person or any other kind of load on his back.

"But when you make horses work, you have to put something on their feet to protect them. Way, way back, somebody figured out a metal horseshoe to help them."

"How long do horses leave their shoes on?" Bert asked.

Sam said that a horse should be shod about once

a month. The outside wall of his foot grows the way a fingernail does. This has to be filed down so the old shoe will fit, or else new shoes have to be put on.

"But you'll see all this at Rufus's," Sam concluded.

As they neared the blacksmith shop, the boys could hear a loud *clang, clang*. Rufus was busy hammering a horseshoe into the shape he wanted it.

Sam introduced the boys and Rufus said he was glad to see them. He was very big and had a face which seemed to be smiling all the time.

"I'm mighty glad Sam brought you over," he said. "He's been telling me about the Bobbsey twins for years."

Next to the anvil on which Rufus was hammering the horseshoe was a round brick fireplace with a roaring blaze in it. Freddie was fascinated as he watched Rufus pick up a horseshoe in a pair of tongs, hold it down in the fire a few moments, and lay it back on the anvil. Then he hammered the shoe a little more. After he repeated this two or three times, he put the horseshoe aside to cool.

"Sam, do you want to bring Mollie in?" the blacksmith asked.

The boys wondered who Mollie was and why she was in a blacksmith's shop. A moment later they both grinned, as Sam led in a large white horse.

"Mollie's going to be in the parade," Rufus told them. "I have to be sure that her shoes fit exactly."

While he was hunting for new horseshoe nails of the proper length, Rufus said to Sam, "Will you see if the frogs are all right?"

Freddie looked around the shop. He did not see any frogs, and wondered if they were outside. Hurrying out of the door, he again looked all around. There were no frogs in sight and no water in which they might be living. He returned to Rufus.

"Where are the frogs?" he asked.

The blacksmith chuckled. "Why, on Mollie," he replied.

Freddie walked up to the big white horse and looked all over her. There was no sign of a frog. Turning to Sam, he said:

"Are you playing a joke on me?"

"Why, of course not," Sam replied. "The frog's under Mollie's foot. Suppose you lift it up and find out for yourself."

Freddie lifted Mollie's left hind leg and looked. There was no frog hidden there.

By this time the two men and Bert were laughing. Finally Bert said, "I guess we've kept you guessing long enough, Freddie. Tell him, Sam."

Sam explained that the triangular-shaped flesh on the bottom of a horse's foot is known as the frog, and Freddie laughed at the way he had been fooled.

"The frogs act as a cushion when a horse is travelling," Sam went on. "If he's properly shod, the frog touches the ground. But sometimes a blacksmith is careless and makes the shoe too deep. Then the poor horse becomes lame."

Bert spoke of the collection of horseshoes at the lodge and remarked that they were all of different sizes and heights.

"Well, horses' feet are just about as different as human beings' feet," said Sam. "That's why they have to have different kinds of shoes.

"And more than that, the kinds of shoes depend on what a horse is going to do. A saddle horse or one that's going to pull a fancy wagon wears heavy shoes and has longer toes so he can show off better. But racehorses wear light racing plates, just heavy enough to last for the one race."

Freddie sighed. What a lot there was to learn about horse-shoeing!

Rufus walked over now with the cooled-off shoes to put on Mollie. As he nailed them in place, he said:

"In the wintertime we put special pegs on the shoes to keep the horses from slipping on snow and ice. Say, Freddie, how would you like to put a few of these nails in place?"

The little boy was thrilled by this idea. Mollie was gentle and permitted the change of blacksmiths without fuss. Freddie was very careful and managed to hammer in three of the nails.

Bert also took a turn at this job. Then the boys said they must go to meet their family at the restaurant. By the time they reached the Robin's Egg, Mrs. Bobbsey and the girls had finished eating.

"We were so starved we couldn't wait," Nan told her brothers.

Their mother said she wanted to do a little shopping and would leave the boys to order their own lunch. She and the girls would meet them at the lodge.

It was about two o'clock when Bert and Freddie finished their lunch. Bert bought two flashlights, and then the brothers walked up the street to the old hotel. As they went into the hall, the boys gasped. Danny Rugg was there talking to Ben Stillman!

"You've got to let me look through the lodge," Danny was saying to the caretaker. "You've got to unlock the doors and let me look around."

"I'll do nothing of the sort," Ben Stillman replied.

"You will too!" Danny cried. "I'm here for the celebration and visitors can see any place they want to, and I want to see the famous horseshoes. You show them to me!"

"Get out!" the caretaker exclaimed suddenly, his eyes blazing.

"You'd better, Danny," Freddie called out.

Danny turned around. Seeing the Bobbsey boys, he sneered. "Who's talking?" he said.

"What do you want?" Bert said, placing the flashlights on the hall table. "If Mr. Stillman says you can't look around in the lodge, you can't!"

"We live here," said Freddie stoutly. "You get out of our house!"

"I will not!" Danny yelled.

"If you don't, I'm going to call a policeman," Freddie threatened. "You took the riddle note out of the stage-coach and you had no business to."

Danny's eyes narrowed. The next instant he doubled up his fist, pulled back his arm and aimed a blow at Freddie.

CHAPTER XV

A MYSTERIOUS DOOR

"LEAVE my brother alone!" Bert cried out, as Danny Rugg's punch toppled Freddie to the floor.

"He says I took the riddle note from the stagecoach and I didn't!" Danny stated defiantly, and gave Freddie a shove as the smaller boy got up from the floor. At that instant, Bert punched Danny so hard that Danny landed against the stairway.

"Hey, cut that out!" Ben Stillman shouted. "If you want to fight, go outdoors."

The two Bobbseys ran out to the front yard, so that the larger boy would have to follow them. He did, and as soon as he reached the yard, Danny aimed a blow at Bert's head. Bert dodged and came up with a punch which landed on Danny's shoulder.

"Hit him again, Bert!" Freddie urged.

But suddenly Danny grabbed Bert around the middle, pulled him to the ground and tried to sit on him. In the tussle which followed, Freddie suddenly yelled:

113

"The riddle note, Bert! I have it! It dropped out of Danny's pocket!"

Freddie clutched a dirty piece of paper he had picked up. Danny stopped fighting and started to run. But Bert grabbed him by the shirt.

"You said you didn't take that note!" he said.

"And I didn't," Danny replied. "It was——" He stopped speaking, but Bert knew Danny had been about to accuse his friend, Jack Westley. "Oh, keep your old note!" Danny cried scornfully.

Pulling away from Bert, the boy ran down the street. He almost bumped into Mrs. Bobbsey and the girls, who were just returning. Freddie told them what had happened.

"I'm glad we have the note back," Nan said. "Danny's horrible."

"I learned at the bank," said Mrs. Bobbsey, "that Mr. Hall is away. As soon as he returns to town, he'll get in touch with us and we'll show the note to him."

"Mother," said Nan, "don't you think it would be all right for me to try the glue dissolvent on just one door? Mr. Dickson asked me to, and he's going to inherit the hidden money if it can be found."

Mrs. Bobbsey thought a moment. Then she said she believed Nan had better wait, since Mr. Hall would be back soon. "Why don't we just do some exploring without opening doors?" she suggested.

"I bought two flashlights downtown," Bert announced. "Let's start being detectives right now."

His mother nodded and once more they entered the gloomy corridor that led from the wing to the old lodge. Nan, holding one of the lights, led the way. Bert took the other and brought up the rear.

"Maybe this time we'll solve the horseshoe riddle," his twin said hopefully.

"I have an idea it isn't going to be easy," their mother answered.

They walked to the lobby and then beyond into an adjoining dark corridor. Suddenly Nan stopped short and began to sniff. She thought she smelled something familiar, which had a very pungent odour. Now Nan was certain she had smelled it before and became very excited.

"I know!" she cried. "I smell the glue dissolvent!"

The others sniffed hard too. Then Flossie said her sister was right.

"But where is it coming from?" Mrs. Bobbsey asked.

Nan and Bert flashed their lights about, and Nan walked a little way ahead. The odour was growing stronger.

Now positive that someone had been using the dissolvent, she ran the full length of the corridor. Reaching the very last door on the street side, she discovered the source of the odour. The door reeked of it!

"Here it is!" she called, and the others ran up.

Then suddenly a frightening idea came to Nan.

The ghost of Horseshoe Lodge might be on the other side of the door!

She whispered her thought to Mrs. Bobbsey, who said she would try the door, and told the children to stand back. Taking Bert's light, she turned the knob and pushed against the door. Slowly it swung open and she flashed the light around. No one was revealed.

"This is very strange," she declared. "We had better ask Mr. Stillman what he knows about it."

"Please wait a minute, Mother," Nan begged. "I'll run up to my bedroom and see if someone took my bottle of dissolvent."

Nan hurried away. Reaching her room, she took her suit-case from the closet and opened it. The bottle of glue dissolvent was still in the bag and not one drop was gone! Completely puzzled, Nan dashed down the stairs and returned to her family.

"Nobody used any of the dissolvent in my bottle," she said. "So somebody must have taken some from Mr. Dickson's shop and used it on this door!"

"And maybe found the gold already," Flossie added in a worried voice, "and—and taken it away!"

"Then he's got to give it back!" Freddie declared.

Mrs. Bobbsey thought that as long as the door already had been unsealed, it would be all right to look around the room. Evidently it had once been the owner's private office, but there was little in it now—just an old-fashioned roll-top desk and a few chairs.

"Nothing seems to have been disturbed," Mrs. Bobbsey remarked.

"Maybe we scared away whoever it was," Nan suggested.

"That's possible," agreed Mrs. Bobbsey. "In any case, we should tell Mr. Stillman about it."

Bert offered to get the caretaker. When Ben arrived, he was amazed to hear what had happened.

"I can't figure out how anybody could get in," he said. "I keep my front door locked when I'm not at home, and the other doors are boarded up."

He opened the roll-top desk and pulled out all the drawers. There was nothing in any of them. The closet also was empty.

"I'm sure the bad man found the gold and took it away," Flossie said in disappointment.

Bert had another idea. He flashed his light around and made certain the only footprints on the dusty floor were those of himself and the others in the room. To make sure, he had each one walk in the tracks he had made.

The twins spent most of the afternoon looking for footprints and secret entrances. But they found nothing to show where a burglar had entered.

"He must have walked through the air," Flossie remarked.

Late in the afternoon Mrs. Bobbsey called the

children to get ready for supper. They would meet their father downtown, she said, and eat together.

When they met Mr. Bobbsey and he saw Freddie's excited face, he said:

"I can see that my Little Fireman has a lot to tell me. What happened today?"

Freddie told about the mysteriously unglued door and about the missing sapphire. Mr. Bobbsey's face became serious. "If someone has stolen some of Mr. Dickson's dissolvent, he might learn how to make it himself to sell," he said. "We must do something about it at once. I'll phone Mr. Dickson and find out as soon as we reach the restaurant."

He led the way into a pleasant tea-room called the Blue Door and chose a table near a front window. The twins and their mother sat down, and Mr. Bobbsey went to a telephone booth in the rear. Mrs. Bobbsey was just reading the menu aloud to Freddie and Flossie, when suddenly Freddie grabbed his twin's arm.

"Flossie, look! That man across the street! He's the one who tried to take the glue away from Mr. Dickson!"

CHAPTER XVI

A PUZZLING DAY

"YOU mean that's Will Hemp?" Bert asked excitedly, looking out of the restaurant window.

"Yes," Freddie and Flossie answered together.

Bert got up from the table and started for the door. "I'll get him!" he cried.

Nan dashed after her brother. But by the time they reached the street, the suspect had turned the corner and was out of sight.

"Hurry!" Nan called to her twin, who was considerably in the lead. "Don't lose him!"

Bert rushed to the side street but the man was gone.

"Oh, where did he go?" Nan cried, as she reached her brother.

Just then they spotted Will Hemp coming from a store and rushed after him. The man began walking very fast, but suddenly he realized there were running footsteps behind him. Turning, he saw the children coming and waited.

"Do you want me?" he asked, smiling.

Bert and Nan were astonished. This man certainly did not act like a thief!

"Why—er—yes," Bert said. "Aren't you **Mr. Will Hemp?**"

At this question the man stopped smiling and wanted to know why they thought he was. Embarrassed, Bert said that his younger brother and sister had thought they had identified him.

"And who are you?" the man asked.

"Why, I'm Bert Bobbsey," the boy replied.

"Well, I'm sorry to disappoint you," the man said. "I must look like somebody named Will Hemp. But I'm not Hemp. Good-bye."

He turned about and walked off. Bert and Nan looked at each other, feeling very foolish. Slowly they returned to the restaurant.

"Did you catch him?" Freddie asked.

"It was the wrong man," Bert reported.

"Oh, I was sure that was the bad man," said Flossie. Then she added, "Didn't he have a funny looking scar on his forehead?"

"Why, yes, he did," said Nan. Then a frown crossed her face. "That was Will Hemp, all right. Only he wouldn't tell us so. Bert, we let him get away!"

Flossie sighed. "More bad luck," she said.

When Mr. Bobbsey returned to the table, he was amazed to hear that Will Hemp was in town.

"That makes what I just heard from George Dickson even more probable," he said.

He went on to tell his family that someone had broken into the Dickson shop and stolen a quantity of both the glue and the dissolvent. Dickson himself felt sure it was Will Hemp who had done this.

"Dad," said Bert quickly, "shouldn't we tell the police?"

"Yes, and we will," his father replied.

Once more he went to the telephone, and this time talked to the sergeant on duty at the police station. The officer assured Mr. Bobbsey that all policemen would be told to look for a man with a bad scar on his forehead. "And tell your children if they see Hemp again, to hold on to him," the sergeant added. "He may know something about that sapphire Ben Stillman told us was stolen."

After Mr. Bobbsey delivered the message, Nan asked him how Mrs. Dickson and her little girl were. "Are they still in the hospital?" she inquired.

"They're a little better," Mr. Bobbsey reported, "but they'll be there for some time. Poor Mr. Dickson is very worried about them and about his bills."

"We just have to find his gold real soon," said Flossie.

The Bobbseys returned to Horseshoe Lodge. Just as they entered the caretaker's wing of the building, there came the sound of a thud from the pitch-black lobby beyond the door.

"You children stay here," their father ordered. "I'll get a flashlight and see what has happened."

Bert quickly brought a light to him. Mr. Bobbsey opened the door and strode along the dark corridor, beaming his light from side to side. Finally he called to the twins. When they reached him, he pointed to the wall where the horseshoes were hanging.

"A couple of them fell off the wall," he said.

Two large horseshoes lay on the floor, though the nails on which they had hung were firmly in place.

"What do you think made them fall down?" Nan asked.

"I wish I knew," her father answered. "This is strange—very strange indeed. Well, children, I think we'd better go back to our wing before anything else happens here."

The twins soon said good night to their parents and went to bed. But they could not help wondering whether, during the night, the person who had used the glue dissolvent would come back. And if he did, would he be Will Hemp?

Despite their thoughts, the twins slept soundly. In the morning Mrs. Bobbsey said she would like to try a different restaurant for breakfast this time, so they went to one which had booths along two sides of it. She and Mr. Bobbsey seated themselves in one with the small twins, while Nan and Bert sat down in a booth opposite. When the waitress came up to them, she looked from one set of twins to the other, then asked:

"Are you by any chance the Bobbseys?"

"Yes, we are," the twins' mother replied.

"Then you're just the people a man was looking for."

"What do you mean?" Mr. Bobbsey asked her.

The waitress explained that the day before, a man had come in and asked her whether the Bobbsey twins ever ate in this restaurant. When she told him no, he had said he wanted very much to talk to them.

"Why?" Freddie asked.

"He didn't tell me, but he said it was very important," the girl replied.

"Who was he?" Mr. Bobbsey asked.

"I don't know," the waitress said. "But he certainly seemed anxious to get hold of you. Oh!" she exclaimed, looking towards the door, "here he comes now!"

CHAPTER XVII

THE WALKING KNIGHT

A TALL grey-haired man wearing glasses walked directly towards the Bobbsey family. The waitress looked at him and said:

"Here are the people you were looking for."

"That's fine," he said, smiling. "You are the Bobbseys?" When the children's father nodded, the man continued, "I've been searching all over town for your twins."

"Won't you sit down?" Mr. Bobbsey asked.

The man walked over to get a chair and carried it to the booths where the family was sitting.

"Let me introduce myself," he said. "I'm Harry Cowan and I have the honour of being chairman of the 175th anniversary celebration.

"As you know," Mr. Cowan went on, "we are trying to have the best celebration we have ever had in Bartley."

Mr. Bobbsey said, "So I've heard."

"The committee has arranged a long and very

124

fine parade," Mr. Cowan said. "There will be all sorts of floats, and a stage-coach——"

Putting his hand on Mr. Cowan's arm, Freddie said, "We know there's going to be a stage-coach in the parade. We rode to Bartley in it."

"Yes, yes," Mr. Cowan said, smiling. "I know that, and it's the reason I'm here. I'd like it very much, Mr. and Mrs. Bobbsey, if you would permit your twins to ride in it in the parade."

"Oh boy!" Freddie shouted. "That's swell."

"What do you think, Mrs. Bobbsey?" Mr. Cowan asked.

The twins' mother smiled. "With all the children there are in Bartley, I feel it is a great honour that you should ask my twins."

"Not at all, not at all," the committee chairman said. "Some friends of mine in Lakeport told me how well your children conducted themselves while driving through the main street. I decided then and there they were just the ones to ride in the coach."

He went on to say that a Miss Daisy Fairweather had costumes to hire. If Mrs. Bobbsey would take the twins to Miss Fairweather's home, she would select the proper clothes for them to wear in the parade.

"I'll be very glad to," Mrs. Bobbsey said. "Where does she live?"

"At 17 Cherry Street," Mr. Cowan replied.

He arose from the chair and shook hands with Mr. and Mrs. Bobbsey.

"I understand that a man named Sam who works for you has a costume already and could act as footman. Will you please ask him to ride with the twins?"

"Yes, I'll speak to him," Mr. Bobbsey replied.

Looking at Bert, Mr. Cowan asked, "I plan to drive the stage-coach myself. Would you like to sit up front with me?"

"Yes, I would, sir, very much," Bert replied.

"Mr. Cowan," Flossie spoke up, "would you like my old-fashioned suit-case to carry on top of the coach?"

"That would be fine," Mr. Cowan said. "Bring it with you the day of the parade."

After he left, the children began to talk excitedly about riding in the stage-coach and what they would wear.

"It won't be long before you'll know," their mother laughed.

The Bobbseys ate their breakfast, then the twins went with their mother to Miss Daisy Fairweather's house. Miss Fairweather was a plump, pleasant woman with a great deal of blonde hair piled high on her head. After Mrs. Bobbsey told her why they had come, she opened the door wide, inviting them inside.

The twins were amazed at Miss Fairweather's house. It was not like any place they had ever seen.

Along all the walls were large glass showcases filled with costumes of every variety. Seeing the children's look of interest, Miss Fairweather explained that she had once been a wardrobe mistress at an opera house.

"I took care of all the costumes for the singers," she said. "When the clothes got a little old or were not to be used again for one reason or another, I bought them cheap. That's how I started my collection and I've added to it for years. Would you like to look at some of the things?"

"Oh yes," they answered.

Miss Fairweather pointed out various costumes, asking Bert and Nan if they could identify any of them from their study of history.

"That's a Roman soldier's," Bert identified one.

"Right," Miss Fairweather said.

"And that's like what Queen Elizabeth wore in 1600," Nan said, noticing a tight-fitting red velvet dress with a high ruching at the neck.

"I see a Puritan's," Flossie said, pointing.

"You're both right," said Miss Fairweather. "I think something you may not know is that children in olden times wore clothes which looked exactly like their mother's and father's."

She showed Bert and Freddie the fancy kind of hats boys used to wear, and the brothers chuckled.

"I'm glad we don't have to wear them now," said Freddie.

"I'll tell you something even worse which girls

in olden times had to wear," said the costume mistress. "Corsets!"

"What!" Nan cried.

"That's right," said Miss Fairweather. "I'll show you."

In one of the cases was a bright yellow skirt with a white blouse and a black lace corset which went over it.

"It was the style to have a very slim waistline," Miss Fairweather explained, "and this was the way they accomplished it. And girls and women wore many, many petticoats, too. Sometimes as many as twelve."

"I won't have to wear something like that in the parade, will I?" Flossie asked fearfully.

"I'm afraid your little waist could never stand it," Miss Fairweather laughed. "And how those poor ladies ever managed their bulky clothes in the olden days I don't know. They had to walk sideways through doors and when they sat down their wide skirts covered a whole couch!"

Freddie, who had said little up to this moment, suddenly called out, "I'm glad I'm a boy."

"That wouldn't have helped you any if you had lived in the eighteenth century," Miss Fairweather told him. "You would have had to wear a wig, your face would have been rouged and powdered, and you would have had big buckles and high heels on your shoes."

Freddie made a face, then suddenly an idea

struck him. "Will I have to be fixed up like that in the parade?" he asked. "If I do, I'm not going to be in it."

"Oh, I'll find you something simpler," Miss Fairweather promised. "But before I get your costume, I want to show all of you one more thing."

She led them to still another room. In the centre of the floor stood the model of a knight in full armour. She explained that figures like this were often used in operas.

"I like that costume," said Freddie. "You could be all covered up when you went to war and carry a sword and everything."

He continued to gaze at it even when the others followed Miss Fairweather to another room where she kept the costumes she rented. Freddie walked round and round the knight in armour. He wondered where the sword that went with it might be.

He spied several swords in a showcase along the wall. He ran over to it and tried to open the case. It was locked, but he continued to stand there and gaze at the weapons.

Suddenly the little boy heard a noise behind him and turned abruptly. His hair almost stood on end. The knight was moving towards him!

"Don't!" Freddie shrieked, thinking the soldier was going to attack him.

He looked at the door and wondered if he could get out in time.

"Stop!" the figure said in a deep voice.

Freddie stood still, a prickling sensation running up and down his spine. Then, as he gazed wide-eyed, he heard a giggle behind the knight. The next moment Bert poked his head from behind the figure and said:

"Want to fight?"

Freddie laughed too, and helped Bert shove the knight back in place. Then they went into the other room where Mrs. Bobbsey was helping the girls pick out costumes.

"I think your sons will have to wear knee breeches, long stockings and buckled shoes after all," Miss Fairweather was saying. "And they'll have to put on wigs too."

"Oh, no!" cried Freddie.

Nan was given a pale green dress with a full skirt and a large yellow hat with a white plume on it. Her sister's costume was made almost completely of ruffles of white lace over a blue silk petticoat. Like Nan's it had a very full skirt. Flossie would wear a black velvet bonnet with blue ribbons which tied under her chin.

"I'm sure you'll all look adorable," said Miss Fairweather, as she packed the costumes into boxes for them to carry away.

"I'll wave to you from the stage-coach," said Flossie, as they bade Miss Fairweather good-bye.

"I'll be looking for you," she smiled.

When they reached Horseshoe Lodge, the

Bobbseys took their packages upstairs. As Flossie walked into the room she shared with Nan, the little girl noticed that her suit-case was not standing by the wall where she had left it.

"Nan, did you take my bag?" she asked.

"No."

Flossie asked her brothers. They both said they had not touched it. She ran to her mother's room to find out.

"Why no, dear," said Mrs. Bobbsey. "I didn't move it."

They all started a search, but the bag was not in sight. Flossie had just started to say, "Oh dear, what'll I do?" when Nan suddenly cried out:

"All our bags are gone!"

"What do you mean?" Bert asked in amazement.

Nan said she had suddenly realized that none of the Bobbseys' suit-cases were around.

"They must have been stolen!" she exclaimed.

CHAPTER XVIII

THE GHOST

"ARE all our clothes stolen too?" Flossie cried out.

She rushed to the closet in her room to look for hers. The dresses still hung there. Flossie hurried to the bureau and opened it. Her underthings had not been disturbed.

"I guess the thief only took our bags," she said. "But I want my old-fashioned suit-case back!" the little girl wailed.

Nothing had been taken from the other rooms, either, except the bags. Mrs. Bobbsey decided to go downstairs at once and ask Ben Stillman if he knew anything about the theft. The caretaker was just coming in the front door. He shook his head in amazement when he heard what had happened.

"I had to go downtown," he said. "And I'm afraid that for once I left the door unlocked. Someone must have come in."

At this moment Nan came rushing down the stairway. She had just looked out of a window, she

said, and thought she had seen one of the missing
suit-cases under a bush.

"I'm going to look," she added.

The others followed her outside. Under the
bush was Mr. Bobbsey's suit-case!

"I guess the thief couldn't carry all our bags at
once, so he left Dad's," Freddie suggested.

Bert thought this was probably true and that
more of the bags might be hidden about the
property. The twins scattered and began a search.
Within a few minutes all the luggage had been
found but Flossie's suit-case.

"I don't believe the person planned to steal the
bags at all," said Bert. "I think somebody was
playing a joke on us."

"You mean Danny Rugg?" Freddie asked.

"I'm sure he's the one," Bert replied.

"But what does he want with my suit-case?"
Flossie asked.

The others could not answer this, but Mrs.
Bobbsey thought they should continue their search.
Perhaps the bag would turn up.

"Say, maybe Danny's hiding around here hoping
to find the gold," Bert told Nan.

"Then let's hunt for him," his twin urged.

At this moment Flossie called out that she had
found her missing plaid bag. It had been hidden
in the barn.

The children returned to the house and Bert
told his twin he would get the two flashlights so

they could search in the closed-up part of the lodge for Danny. As they were ready to start, Ben Stillman came out of his quarters.

"One of the sheets is gone from my bed," he said crossly. "Did you children take it?"

"Certainly not," said Bert. "But maybe the same person who hid the bags took the sheet."

Ben Stillman shrugged, went back into his apartment and closed the door. Bert and Nan looked at each other.

"Say," said Bert, "maybe Danny's going to play ghost and try to scare us."

Nan giggled. "Let's turn the tables on him!"

The twins opened the door to the hallway which led to the lobby of the old hotel. Tiptoeing along and flashing the lights ahead of them, they listened for any sound. There was not one and they began to think they were wrong about Danny being in the lodge.

Upon reaching the lobby, the twins decided to separate. Nan walked down the far corridor alone. Bert began to study the lobby floor carefully, looking for footprints. He had barely started to do this when Nan cried out:

"Bert! Come here! Quick!"

Her twin dashed down the corridor. Nan was staring into old Mr. Dickson's private office. Suddenly a figure burst through the doorway and pushed her roughly aside. It was Danny Rugg!

The boy had a wild, frightened look in his eyes.

He rushed up the corridor. Bert grabbed hold of him.

"Where are you going, Danny?" he asked.

"Let me go! Let me go! Quick!" Danny cried fearfully. "There's a ghost in there!"

"Where?" Bert demanded.

He did not let go of Danny, although the boy tried hard to get away.

"In—in there," Danny stuttered.

By this time Nan had reached the boys. The twins marched Danny back to the office and beamed their lights around. There was no one in the room and no sign of anything resembling a ghost. They began to laugh.

"You were seeing things, Danny," Bert told him. "It serves you right for hiding our suit-cases."

"I—I was only having fun," said Danny, who was still trembling. "I tell you I did see a ghost."

"Well, where did he go?" Bert asked.

"I d-don't know," Danny said. "But I can explain about the bags." He said he had come to see the Bobbseys and to ask them to show him the lodge since Ben Stillman would not do it.

"The door was open and no one was at home, so I came in," Danny went on. "I decided to play a joke on you and hide your suit-cases."

"What about the sheet you took?" Nan asked.

Danny looked blank. "Sheet?" he asked. "I don't know anything about a sheet."

It was the twins' turn to look surprised. They told Danny it had been taken from the caretaker's bed.

Suddenly Bert had an idea. Maybe Danny *had* seen a "ghost"—at least someone who was playing the part of a ghost and wearing the sheet from Ben Stillman's bed.

"Tell us just what you saw," Bert said to Danny.

"Well," the boy began, "I didn't have any flashlight so I had to be real careful. I tried all the doors, but none of them would open until I came to this one. There was a candle burning on top of the desk, so I decided to look around."

"There isn't any candle here now," said Bert, beaming his flashlight on top of the desk.

Danny began to quiver. "Then the ghost t-took the candle!" he whimpered. "I want to get out of here!"

"Nothing doing," said Bert, grabbing Danny's arm again. "Tell us what happened."

"I—I was standing right here by the desk, when all of a sudden there was a ghost standing in front of me," Danny said. "He didn't make a sound and he didn't say anything. Just pointed towards the door."

Danny said he had been so frightened he had backed into the desk chair, pushing it along the floor.

"I guess that's the noise I heard when I yelled for you, Bert," said Nan.

"Yeah, I guess so," said Danny. "Then suddenly the candle went out and I started to run."

"What did the ghost look like?" Bert asked.

"I could only see his eyes and forehead," Danny replied. "His eyes were awful; just like fire. And he had a funny looking red scar on his forehead."

Danny suddenly broke away from Bert, snatched Nan's flashlight from her hand, and dashed out of the door.

"Let him go," said Bert. "You and I will find out more about this ghost business, Nan."

"You think Will Hemp was playing ghost?" Nan asked her brother.

"I sure do," said Bert. "Let's find out how he got out of this room."

He beamed his light all over the walls and the two children pushed and tapped on them, hoping to find a secret panel. But they could not locate anything which would move.

"It must be in the floor," Bert decided.

The twins inspected every one of the wide, old-fashioned floor-boards. Suddenly Bert exclaimed:

"Look, Nan! I think this section is a trapdoor."

He ran his toe up one section of board, across the end of it, up the next one and across.

"Help me pull it up," he asked his sister, starting to tug.

Nan stopped him. "Please don't," she begged. "We must get somebody else first. Come on, we'll find Ben Stillman and he can open it with us."

CHAPTER XIX

GLUED IN

"QUICK! Mr. Stillman!" Nan cried, knocking on the door of the caretaker's apartment.

Ben opened the door, plainly annoyed at being disturbed.

"Please come with us," Nan begged. "We think the man who stole Mr. Dickson's glue dissolvent is right here in the lodge. He took your sheet and put it on to scare Danny Rugg."

"Nonsense!" Ben Stillman said. Nevertheless, he left his apartment and followed the twins across the hall, through the door and down the dark corridor.

Bert quickly led the way into the old private office of the lodge.

"I'm sure there's a trapdoor here," he said, pointing to the floor. "We want to go down to the cellar and find out if that man's hiding there."

"In that case, I'll go down alone," said Ben Stillman firmly.

He tried to lift the trapdoor which Bert had indicated, but it was too heavy for him. There was no ring or handle, and it was necessary to squeeze one's fingers into the cracks between the boards.

"I'll help you," Bert offered.

Together the two of them managed to tilt the trapdoor. Slowly it swung upwards, revealing steep, narrow, stone steps to the floor below. The caretaker stared unbelievingly, then flashed Bert's light around. There was nothing in sight.

"Let's go down and look carefully," Bert proposed.

Ben Stillman grunted, and started down the steps. The twins waited till he reached the bottom, then Bert went down with Nan following him.

The cubbyhole was about ten feet square and contained only a large pile of logs. But Nan saw something white stuffed among the logs and pulled it out.

"Here's the 'ghost's' sheet," she said, holding it up. "Is this the one from your bed, Mr. Stillman?"

The caretaker examined the sheet and said it was. For the first time he became really interested in the children's story. He searched the walls carefully, but there was no other entrance to the cubbyhole.

"Oh dear, the ghost is gone!" Nan said. "But how did he get out?"

Ben Stillman looked at her in disgust. "He got out when you came for me, of course. Nuisance!"

The trio had just turned to leave, when they heard quick-moving footsteps overhead. Suddenly the trapdoor above them crashed down.

Ben Stillman ran up the steps and pushed against it, but the door would not open. A frantic look came over the man's face.

"Let me help," said Bert and threw his weight against the door.

A familiar odour came to Nan's nostrils. She cried out that Mr. Dickson's glue had been used on the trapdoor!

"We'll never get out of here!" she wailed.

For a second the others agreed with her, then Ben Stillman said, "The glue couldn't set that quickly. Come on, Bert, heave ho!"

The two shoved with all their might and Nan pushed too. Their combined efforts finally began to break the slowly sealing glue and the trapdoor was pushed up slowly.

"We're going to get out!" Nan exclaimed. Tears of joy came to her eyes.

There was no sign of the "ghost" in the office above, and they concluded he had left the lodge. The three hurried back to the wing and Ben Stillman put in a call to the police.

"We need a policeman here night and day to watch this place," he stated. "Something mighty funny is going on."

He hung up abruptly and said good-bye to Bert and Nan. As the twins started up the stairs, their

father came in. At once they told him what had
happened and Mr. Bobbsey looked alarmed.

"That 'ghost' is dangerous," he exclaimed.
"You children stay out of his way. No more trips
to the cellar."

"All right," Nan promised.

The twins went upstairs to their rooms. Some
time later they heard their names called. When
they came down they found a young policeman
named Murtry who had been sent to find out what
had happened. He asked the twins to show him
where the trapdoor was, and the room below it.

This time Freddie and Flossie came along, and
Mrs. Bobbsey also. All of them gazed in amazement at the strange-looking trapdoor and the
cubbyhole under the office.

"This situation is more serious than the police
department thought," said Policeman Murtry,
frowning.

The twins stayed to talk with him for a while,
then went back to their own part of the lodge.

About noontime Joy Lambert came to see them.
She asked if they had been having a good time.

"We've had an awful scary time," said Flossie.
"My brother and sister almost caught a ghost this
morning."

"What!" Joy cried.

"Yes," Nan told her. "And the ghost almost
glued us into the cellar."

Joy asked what in the world they were talking

about. When she heard the story, she looked serious.

"Goodness," she said. "If my father had ever known what was going to happen, he never would have suggested your staying here. Well," she went on, "I came to tell you about something nice. I'm going to have a party this afternoon, and I want you all to come.

"There's going to be a big surprise," Joy added, her eyes twinkling.

CHAPTER XX

THE MAGICIAN'S CLUE

"WHAT'S the surprise?" Flossie asked Joy Lambert.

"I'm not going to tell you," the older girl laughed. "You have to come to my party and find out for yourself."

Nan inquired what time the party was. Upon learning that it was to start at three o'clock, she said they would all be there. After Joy had gone the younger twins began to guess what the surprise might be.

"I'll bet it's a new kind of game," Flossie suggested.

"Maybe it's a pony ride," Freddie offered.

"Or flag ice-cream," his twin giggled.

"What's that?" Freddie wanted to know. He had never heard of such a thing.

"It's red, white and blue," Flossie replied.

Freddie scoffed at this. "Who ever heard of blue ice-cream?" he demanded.

"I have," said Flossie. "The red is raspberry ice. The white's vanilla and the blue's made out of huckleberries."

"I wouldn't like it," said Freddie. "I hope the surprise is better than that."

At two o'clock, after a quick lunch at a nearby sandwich shop, the children began to dress for the party. As Flossie looked at the box which held her costume for the parade, she said:

"I wish I could wear this, Nan. Do you think it would be all right?"

"Oh, no," her sister answered. "We mustn't let anyone see what we're going to wear. And we mustn't tell, either."

Flossie promised. Then she took out a white dress with pink and blue flowers embroidered on it, saying she would wear this for the party. Nan put on a two-piece linen dress.

"You both look very sweet," said Mrs. Bobbsey, coming into the room. "Do you think you can find your way alone to Joy Lambert's house?"

Nan assured her mother they could. In a few moments the boys were ready and the twins set off. Since Nan was leading the way, the others paid no attention to the route she was taking. After they had walked a long time, Flossie said:

"I didn't know Joy lived so far from Horseshoe Lodge. I'm getting tired."

"We'll be there in a minute," said Nan, turning another corner and walking along farther.

But suddenly she stopped. All the houses on the street looked strange to her. This was not the street Joy Lambert lived in after all!

"I guess we should have turned the other way," Nan said sheepishly.

They went back to the corner, crossed to the other side and walked a distance farther. Then Nan stopped again. She shook her head.

"I guess this isn't right, either," she said.

"Oh, dear," Flossie cried out. "We'll miss the s'prise."

"I believe we should have turned left two blocks back," Nan answered. "Come on, I'll find out."

The twins turned around again and hurried in the other direction. Nan turned down the street she thought was the right one, but in a few moments confessed that Joy did not live on this street either.

"I'm getting awful tired," said Flossie. "I'm going to sit down."

With this she walked up to a porch and seated herself on the steps. A woman came outside and said hello to her.

"We're lost," Flossie stated. "We started for a party, but we can't find it."

The woman smiled and said perhaps she could help them. Whose house were they going to?

Flossie told her and the woman offered to look in the telephone book and find out where the Lamberts lived. When she came back she told the little girl there were three families of Lamberts in

Bartley. Did they want the William Lamberts, the George Lamberts or the Donald Lamberts? Flossie said she did not know but would ask her brothers and sister. Hurrying to where they still stood on the sidewalk, she said:

"Do we want Georges or Donalds or what?"

The others laughed, asking what Flossie meant. When she explained, Nan said:

"I think I remember Mrs. Lambert calling Joy's father Donald."

She walked with Flossie to the porch and told the woman this.

"Well, the Donald Lamberts live on Maple Street," was the reply.

"Oh, I remember now," said Nan. "That was the name on the piece of paper Joy gave me."

She thanked the woman, who gave the children directions, and once more they started off. This time they reached the party. Several boys and girls were playing games in the yard.

The Bobbseys joined in and had a lot of fun for the next hour. But all this time they kept wondering if the surprise was over. Finally Joy clapped her hands for silence.

"Please come inside the house," she invited. "Now we'll have the surprise."

How relieved the Bobbseys were, as all the children scrambled up the porch steps and went into the living-room! When everyone was seated, some on chairs, others on the floor, Joy said:

"Mr. Trillo is going to entertain us. He has lots of tricks. Look out! He may play some on you."

Giggling, Joy sat down on the floor near the door. In walked a man who wore a long black robe. In one hand he held a suit-case and in the other a violin and bow.

He laid the suit-case on the piano and opened it up. The children could not see what was inside. Turning to his young audience, he smiled and said:

"Little ladies and gentlemen, I'm very glad to be here with you today. I shall play for you, but I want you to watch my magic violin carefully."

With that he placed the violin beneath his chin and began to play a pretty melody. It reminded Flossie of birds twittering in the springtime. Suddenly the little girl's eyes nearly popped out of her head. Was she seeing things or were there actually little birds sitting on the violin twittering?

Suddenly the birds disappeared. Mr. Trillo finished the piece and asked if anyone in the audience had a special number he would like played. When no one spoke, he said:

"Well, suppose I play one about a mouse."

He began to play *Three Blind Mice*. As the children watched intently, a little mouse came out of the inside of the violin and began to run around the edge of it.

"Look out!" one little girl cried out. "There's a mouse!"

The mouse disappeared, and Mr. Trillo laughed.

"A mouse?" he said. "Are you sure?"

He turned the violin upside down and peeped inside it, saying he did not see any mouse. He would play again and see if it would come out. Once more he played the tune and immediately the mouse appeared and did a little dance.

But Mr. Trillo did not seem to notice it, and when all the children shrieked that the mouse was there, he stared at them in amazement. He stopped playing and the little animal disappeared. Putting his violin down on the piano, Mr. Trillo said:

"You surely must be mistaken." Then looking directly at Bert Bobbsey, he asked, "Would you like to come up here and play the violin? We'll see if a mouse will come out of it for you."

Bert felt sure the man was going to play some trick on him. But he was game and got up. As he walked forward, Mr. Trillo turned back to the piano and picked up the violin. When Bert reached him, he handed the instrument over, saying:

"Have you ever played a violin?"

"No, I haven't."

"Well, never mind," said Mr. Trillo. "Just pull the bow over the strings and put your fingers anywhere you want. The tune may sound funny but we don't mind. The main thing is to see if the mouse will come out."

Bert tucked the violin under his chin and took

the bow in his hand. He drew it over one of the strings. What a horrible sound it made!

"Goodness!" said Mr. Trillo. "You must play better music than that or certainly no mouse will want to dance to it."

He walked to the other side of the room, as if he thought Bert might play better if the magician were not standing right by him. Bert tried again and pulled the bow even harder over another of the strings. It made an even worse sound than the other one had, but Bert was beginning to enjoy himself, and pulled the bow back and forth.

Suddenly, instead of a mouse appearing on the fiddle, a dog began to whine from inside it. Bert was so amazed that he stopped bowing the strings. He began to laugh and looked over at Mr. Trillo. The magician surely must be making the dog sounds. He was a ventriloquist!

"Let me play that," said Freddie.

He got up and tried to take the violin away from Bert. In the slight tussle which followed, the instrument fell to the floor and several of the children cried out, expecting the violin to be smashed to bits. Instead, the magic instrument bounced off the floor!

Bert and Freddie stood stupefied. But when Mr. Trillo laughed instead of becoming angry, the boys realized that the fiddle was made of rubber. It was stained and varnished to look like a regular violin. Bert handed it back to Mr. Trillo, who said:

"You never could play a regular tune on this. I didn't myself. I changed violins. You children must always watch closely when a magician is at work."

What fun it was! When the show was over, Nan walked up to Mr. Trillo and asked him if he would please play some real music on his violin.

"Why, I'd be very glad to," said the magician. "Have you anything in mind?"

"No, I haven't," Nan replied. "I love all kinds of music."

Most of the children had filed out of the room, but Mr. and Mrs. Lambert and some of the grown-ups who were visiting them stayed to listen. Smiling, the violinist said he would play one of his favourite numbers.

He had played only a few bars, when Nan realized that the tune sounded familiar. She could not recall the name of it and wondered where she had heard it. As Mr. Trillo played on, she suddenly remembered. It was the melody she had heard coming from the fireplace in her room at Horseshoe Lodge!

Nan could hardly wait for Mr. Trillo to finish playing. The instant he bowed the last note, she said to him excitedly:

"Oh, Mr. Trillo, did you play that piece the other night over at the old lodge?"

"Why, no," he replied in surprise. "I just reached Bartley this morning."

Nan told him of the strange happening and asked him what the name of the piece was. He said it was called *Danse Macabre*.

"Some people do not like it because it's rather weird and melancholy," he said. "But it has become generally well known ever since a famous violinist made a very fine recording of it."

"He did?" Nan asked thoughtfully. The violin piece she had heard played that evening might have been from a record!

"But where is the machine?" she thought. "And where was the person who started and stopped the music?"

But these were questions she could not answer, so finally Nan joined the other children outdoors where refreshments were being served.

During the next few hours, however, she kept thinking about the idea of a violin record being played at Horseshoe Lodge. She told her family, and it was the main topic of conversation all through supper. At nine o'clock Ben Stillman reached home. Nan told him that she suspected the mysterious music might have come from a record player.

"Do you know anything about it?" she asked him.

Ben Stillman shook his head. He merely said, "I'm very tired," and went into his apartment.

The old caretaker did not go to bed at once, though. The Bobbsey family had started him thinking about the old lodge. Up to the time of their coming there, nothing had bothered him. But since their arrival they had talked of nothing but ghosts and hidden gold and violin music.

Even though there was a policeman on guard now, Ben Stillman did not feel very comfortable. Perhaps he would not even keep his job. As soon as Mr. Hall returned, he believed he would go down to the bank and tell him that he would not stay any longer.

A couple of hours went by and still the caretaker sat thinking about his problem. Everything was quiet on the second floor. Apparently everyone in the Bobbsey family had gone to bed.

Then suddenly the silence was broken. From somewhere upstairs came a loud cry!

CHAPTER XXI

LIGHTS OUT!

THE old caretaker of Horseshoe Lodge hurried from his apartment and up the stairs to the Bobbseys' rooms. Had something dreadful happened to one of them? Reaching the dimly lit hall above, he met Mrs. Bobbsey dashing from her room.

"What's the matter up here?" he asked her.

"I don't know," she replied, worried, and opened the door to her sons' bedroom.

Ben Stillman followed her inside. They could hear mumbled sounds, then a cry of fear. Mrs. Bobbsey went swiftly to the bed and shook Freddie.

"He's having a nightmare," she explained, and turned on the lamp beside his bed.

Freddie awoke and looked around in a daze. Seeing his mother, he sobbed:

"Oh, I'm glad you're here, Mummy! I was having a dreadful dream."

"I guess you had too much party," Mrs. Bobbsey remarked, smiling. "Now try to go back to sleep and do no more dreaming."

Ben Stillman, standing in the doorway, grunted. "A body can't get any rest around this place," he said. "Well, I'll fix things up for you. I'll get you a horseshoe and hang it in this room."

By this time Bert had awakened. He and his small brother stared at Ben Stillman.

"Why do you want to put a horseshoe in here?" Bert asked him.

"It's supposed to bring good dreams," said Ben Stillman and disappeared.

In a couple of minutes he returned and hung a large horseshoe around one of the posts at the end of the boys' bed.

"Is—is that horseshoe from Mr. Dickson's collection?" Freddie was a little worried.

"No, it's not. It's mine," Ben Stillman replied.

With this he turned on his heel and went downstairs without another word. Mrs. Bobbsey smiled.

"I hope Ben is right about the horseshoe and that you will have good dreams, Freddie." Leaning over, she kissed him good night and said it might help if he thought of nice things as he was going to sleep.

The house was very peaceful during the rest of the night. No one was awakened by any sound, and in the morning Freddie told Bert he had had several nice dreams about horseshoes.

"I dreamed I played a game with you," the little boy chuckled. "And I beat you!"

Bert grinned, asking what else Freddie had dreamed.

"That I was a horse and went to Rufus's to be shod. And lots of real live frogs kept jumping out of my feet."

As soon as Freddie was dressed, he picked up the horseshoe and went downstairs to return it to Ben Stillman. When Freddie told him his dreams about horseshoes, the caretaker gave him one of his rare smiles.

"That's supposed to be good luck," he said. "It means you're going to find unexpected money."

"Really?" Freddie said. "Oh, boy, maybe I'll find the buried gold!" Secretly he decided to become a detective that very morning.

"Well, I hope you do find it," Ben Stillman said. "But if you look around, be careful. The policeman left this morning."

"Why?" Freddie asked.

"Too much to do to get ready for the celebration," the caretaker explained, and added, "Goodbye."

Freddie repeated this news to his family. Mrs. Bobbsey frowned, remarking she thought it was too bad that the old lodge was not better protected.

"Perhaps," Mr. Bobbsey remarked, "the police think that the bank should take care of the property. I'll speak to Mr. Hall about it."

Mr. Bobbsey had received word that Mr. Hall, the banker, would come to see them that evening.

Promptly at eight o'clock the caller arrived for a talk in Mr. and Mrs. Bobbsey's room. Ben Stillman, although invited to come, had said that he had an engagement downtown; and had already gone out.

Mr. Hall was a middle-aged, slightly stout man who had a very pleasant smile. Mr. Bobbsey explained how his family happened to be mixed up in the strange happenings in the lodge. Mr. Hall in turn said he would like very much to have young Mr. Dickson receive the money which his uncle had left him in his will.

"Old George Dickson left a very strange will," the banker went on. "In it he said that this lodge was not to be opened until the riddle about the money had been solved. I've been trying for the past eight months to find out what the riddle is, and where the money is, but the whole thing is as big a mystery as ever."

"I bet the money is right here in the lodge," Freddie said, "and we know what the riddle is. Bert, tell Mr. Hall about the riddle you found in the stage-coach."

Bert got the slip of paper and showed it to Mr. Hall. Then he told the banker how he had found the note in the boot of the old coach while it was being repaired in Lakeport.

"We thought, since the coach belonged in

Bartley," Bert went on, "that the riddle must have something to do with Horseshoe Lodge—I mean," he corrected himself, "Bartley Lodge."

Mr. Hall smiled, saying it was a good nickname for the lodge. He also said he was extremely interested in learning about the riddle.

"I haven't a doubt that it refers to old Mr. Dickson's hidden gold," he exclaimed. "And I believe I can see how it happened."

The only sound in the old-fashioned bedroom was the ticking of an ancient clock as Mr. Hall began his story about the riddle. The Bobbsey twins leaned forward attentively so they would not miss a word.

"Not long before old Mr. Dickson's death," Mr. Hall said, "he rented that stage-coach. Six white horses were hitched to it and the coach was driven to the old lodge. Mr. Dickson announced that he wanted to have his picture taken sitting high on the seat, and holding the reins. He had asked me to come and watch, and he had a photographer sent out from the newspaper.

"After the picture was taken and the old gentleman had climbed down, I found an envelope beside the coach. It was addressed to young Mr. George Dickson, and in one corner a picture of a horseshoe and a violin had been drawn."

"A violin?" exclaimed Nan in surprise.

"Yes, a pretty good drawing. When I handed the envelope to the old gentleman he seemed quite embarrassed. He didn't even thank me, just stuffed the envelope into his pocket.

"At the time I forgot all about it, for he always was a strange sort of man. Now that you tell me about the riddle, I think it must have been in the envelope and dropped by accident inside the boot."

"Old Mr. Dickson probably never knew where he dropped it," Bert guessed. "But why didn't he write another?"

"Undoubtedly because he was taken ill soon after the picture was taken," Mr. Hall said.

Mr. Bobbsey asked Mr. Hall if he knew that young Mr. Dickson had invented a fine glue and also a glue dissolvent. The banker shook his head.

"Mr. Dickson gave me a sample of the dissolvent," Nan told him. "He asked me to use it on the doors here which his uncle had had him glue shut. Would you mind if I tried it, Mr. Hall?"

The banker thought a moment. Then he said:

"I'm just as eager as everyone else to find the money. Suppose I come back Monday morning and we'll get to work on the doors then."

Freddie jumped off his chair in great excitement.

"We know a bad man who's already looking for the gold," he said. "His name is Will Hemp and he has a big scar on his forehead."

"Yes, and he played ghost and scared Danny Rugg," Flossie added.

Mr. Hall frowned. Up to now, he had not really thought there was any money hidden in the lodge. But apparently someone else did, and was trying to get the money for himself.

"We won't let him find the gold," Freddie said staunchly.

The banker smiled. "That's right, Freddie. No dishonest person shall get away with that treasure!"

Mr. Hall said he must leave now. He stood up and the Bobbseys followed him to the door of the bedroom. He had just reached it when all the lights went out.

"Oh, dear, what's the matter?" Flossie asked.

"Just a bulb burned out, I guess," Mrs. Bobbsey said.

But when they stepped into the hall, everyone realized that the whole house was in darkness.

"I guess the trouble is in the fuse box in the cellar," Mr. Bobbsey remarked. "Bert, where are our flashlights?"

"Danny took one, but I'll get the other," Bert said.

When he returned, he lighted the way down the stairs. The Bobbseys all went outside with Mr. Hall. He said good-bye, got into his car, and drove off. Bert then offered to go to the cellar and fix the lights.

"I'd better go along with you," his father said. Turning to the others, he added, "Suppose you all stay outside here until we put the lights on."

The small twins sat down on the steps with their mother, but Nan wandered through the garden at the side of the wing. A street light played faintly on a rose-bush and she went over to smell the flowers.

"They're lovely," Nan thought.

She walked farther in the garden towards the back of the old hotel. Here the ground sloped off sharply, revealing the cellar wall of the lodge. Suddenly she heard a noise.

Turning quickly, Nan was just in time to see a man's figure dart furtively from some bushes close to the wall of the old lodge.

CHAPTER XXII

A TELLTALE NAIL

"MOTHER! Dad! Bert!" Nan shouted. "Come here quick!"

Mr. Bobbsey and Bert did not hear Nan's frantic cry, but Mrs. Bobbsey and the small twins rushed around the side of the house to see what had happened.

"A man!" Nan told them, pointing.

They all ran after him, but by this time he had disappeared around the far corner of the Horseshoe Lodge. When they reached the corner, the man was out of sight.

"He must be running down the street," Nan suggested. "Come on!"

Reaching the sidewalk, they looked in both directions. There was no sign of him.

"That's a shame," Nan said in disappointment.

"Where did he come from?" Mrs. Bobbsey asked.

"I think he was hiding behind some bushes at the back of the lodge," Nan said.

Mrs. Bobbsey said they would get the twins' father and make a search. At this moment lights came on in the wing of the old building and soon Mr. Bobbsey and his son came outside.

"Did I hear shouting?" Mr. Bobbsey asked.

Nan explained about spotting the stranger and said he had run off.

As Bert held the flashlight, Nan led the way towards the bushes where she had first seen the stranger. There were definite footprints around.

"Maybe he was just waiting for a chance to get inside," Mrs. Bobbsey suggested.

Just then Bert gave a shout. The beam of his light had come upon a man's hat. The boy picked it up and looked inside.

"Wow!" he cried. "Here's a clue! Initials in here. W.H.!"

"Will Hemp!" Nan cried out.

"It certainly looks as if you were right," said Mr. Bobbsey, frowning. "It's too bad the man got away."

As they stood silent, wondering what to do next, they heard quiet footsteps coming towards them. Was the person with the initials W.H. returning?

"Perhaps you and the children had better leave," Mr. Bobbsey told his wife.

But before she could move, a man strode into

view. Mr. Bobbsey turned the light on him. Policeman Murtry! He seemed surprised when Freddie
told him they thought the police were not coming
back.

"Not at all," he said.

"You're the rightest man in the world!" Flossie
exclaimed.

The policeman laughed and then asked what
had made her say this.

" 'Cause a burglar's been trying to get into Horseshoe Lodge and we found this hat and we think
it's that bad Will Hemp and you're the right one
to catch him," Flossie replied all in one breath.

Bert handed the hat to the policeman, who
inspected it. "Too bad I got here so late," he said.
"Will Hemp has slipped through our fingers, but
we'll get him!"

"Do you think he'll come back for his hat?" Bert
asked the officer.

"I can't say," Murtry replied. "But I'll be here
waiting for him if he does."

"I wish I could stay with you," said Freddie,
"but I suppose I have to go to bed. Tomorrow
we'll all help you," the little fellow promised.

His mother suggested that, since the next day
was Sunday, they wait until Mr. Hall arrived on
Monday.

Soon after breakfast on Monday morning, the
banker came. He had brought a powerful electric
lantern with him.

"I think it's high time we solved the mystery of the lodge," he said. "Nan, if you will get your bottle of glue dissolvent, we'll start at once."

Nan went upstairs for the bottle, Bert borrowed Ben Stillman's flashlight, and the search began. Young Mr. Dickson had attached a squirt gun to the top of the bottle, so it was easy for Nan to spray the liquid. She stopped at the first door they came to and put some into the cracks.

"Do you think it will really work, Dad, after the glue has been stuck for such a long time?" she asked, worried.

Her father thought it might take several minutes before they would know, and suggested she spray the next door in the meantime. Nan sprayed several before coming back to the first one. Mr. Bobbsey pressed hard against the door, but it would not move. Nan's face fell in disappointment.

"Wait a minute," Mr. Hall said. "The door is probably locked as well as glued."

From his pocket he pulled a large bunch of keys which had been turned over to him when old Mr. Dickson died. One by one the banker tried them in the keyhole without success. At last, however, one fitted. The door clicked. He turned the knob.

The door opened!

"It worked! It worked!" Nan cried gleefully.

The room proved to be a bedroom. It contained the usual pieces of furniture and a rug. All the

Bobbseys and Mr. Hall searched the place carefully, but after a while they had to admit that the hidden gold was not here.

"Let's look in the next room," Freddie urged, dashing into the corridor.

Mr. Hall unlocked this door also and they entered. There was nothing at all in this room, so the searchers did not stay long. On and on they went, ungluing door after door upstairs and downstairs. At last all the doors had been opened but they had found no gold.

"There's not even a violin," Nan sighed.

"No," Mr. Hall agreed. "I believe old Mr. Dickson had a violin, but I think he sold it before he died."

"But *somebody* was playing the violin that night," Nan said, "or else there *is* a record player hidden behind some secret door or sliding panel. Do you know what I think?"

"What?" the others asked her.

"I think it might be behind the wall where the horseshoes hang. Let's go and look at it."

The whole group hurried to the horseshoe collection. As the light played on the faded wallpaper, Nan pointed out that where each horseshoe hung, the paper was less faded.

Suddenly Freddie exclaimed, "There's one horseshoe missing!"

"You're right!" said Bert. "I never noticed that before, did you, Nan?"

Nan admitted that there were so many horseshoes she had not noticed the empty nail. "And look!" she cried, pointing to the horse's name written above it.

"*Fiddle!*" Bert exclaimed. "Nan, do you know what? I'll bet the riddle referred to the horseshoe that belongs here—not to a real fiddle at all."

"That must be it," Nan agreed. "But what do we do now?"

No one could guess. As they stood looking at the empty nail, trying to think what to do next, footsteps came along the corridor and presently Sam joined the group.

"Good morning, everybody," he said cheerfully. "My goodness, I never in all my life saw so many horseshoes outside of a blacksmith shop."

Nan pointed out a few of the famous ones. Then with one finger on the empty nail, she said:

"Sam, if you were going to hide a horseshoe, where would you put it?"

CHAPTER XXIII

THE SECRET BOARD

"IF I was going to hide a special horseshoe, where would I put it?" Sam mused aloud.

He scratched his head, and made a little pattern on the floor with one shoe before answering. Then he grinned.

"I guess I'd put it on a horse's foot," he said. "Why?"

Freddie and Flossie giggled. Flossie told Sam about the horseshoe that was missing from the collection.

"Nan thought it might solve the mystery of Horseshoe Lodge," she said.

"I see," said Sam. "Well, if that shoe got put on a horse's hoof, it sure would be hard to find."

The others agreed, and the small twins were disappointed. Sam now told why he had come to see the Bobbseys. He wanted instructions about the parade.

"We'll meet you at the stage-coach at 1.30," Mr. Bobbsey told him. "And wear your costume."

"Don't let it rain," Flossie begged him.

"I'll do my best," Sam promised.

As he walked off, Flossie and Freddie skipped along beside him. The little girl carried a flashlight to guide them. When they reached the yard, the twins talked to Sam again about where old Mr. Dickson might have hidden the horseshoe they wanted to find.

"Well," he said, "next to putting it on a horse's foot, I'd say a stable would be a good hiding place."

"Oh that *is* a good place," agreed Freddie. "Let's look in the stable."

As Sam left them, Mr. Hall came from the house and said he must get back to the bank. The twins told him what they were going to do and he wished them luck.

"Good-bye! I'll see you later," he called.

In the stable the children began their search in the cleared part of the floor first. Finding nothing, they pulled aside the hay in the various stalls. Still they found nothing.

"I'm going upstairs," Freddie announced, spying a ladder against a side wall. Grasping the rungs, he started to climb.

"Be careful!" Flossie warned him.

At the top of the ladder was a trapdoor leading to the loft above. Freddie managed to push it open and swung himself in.

"Come on up and bring the flashlight," he called to Flossie. "I can't see anything."

Flossie grasped the light and tried to hold it as she climbed the ladder. But the flash completely filled one chubby fist so she had only one hand free to use on the rungs. A moment later one leg swung out. She lost her balance and dropped to the floor.

"Oh!" Flossie cried out.

Freddie poked his head through the opening to see what had happened. Flossie said she could not climb up the ladder and hold the flashlight at the same time. She would have to throw it to her brother.

"Get ready!" she said, swinging her arm back. "One, two, three!"

Flossie threw the light as hard as she could and Freddie reached down as far as he could, but the little boy missed it.

Bang! The light landed on the floor.

"Oo—ee!" Flossie exclaimed, afraid that it was broken.

She picked up the flash and flicked it on.

"Goody!" the little girl said in relief. "It's all right."

Once more she threw the light up to Freddie and this time he caught it. Flossie climbed the ladder. When she reached the top, her twin was waving the light around the loft.

"Do you see anything?" she asked.

"No," Freddie answered, looking dejected. "No violin, no gold, no horseshoes."

"Then let's go downstairs again and look some more," Flossie suggested, and started down the ladder.

Freddie was almost too discouraged to hunt farther, but Flossie kept on. The little girl got down on her hands and knees and began to examine the floor inch by inch. Reaching one of the horse stalls, she made a discovery. One of the floor-boards was loose.

"Look, Freddie," she cried. "Let's pull it up!"

The two children tugged at it. The board was wedged in, but after they yanked on it for several seconds it gave way and came loose.

Beneath it lay a horseshoe!

The twins stared speechless. Then Flossie spoke first.

"We've found it! We've found the missing horseshoe!" she cried, clapping her hands and dancing around.

Freddie grabbed hold of her and jumped up and down in delight. "Let's show the others!" he cried, and the little twins ran out of the barn. What would Bert and Nan say when they saw the horseshoe?

Inside the lodge the older twins were having an adventure of their own. Nan still felt sure there must be a violin hidden somewhere, or else a record player with a record of *Danse Macabre* on it.

"I'm sure it must be somewhere near the chimney to your bedroom, Nan," Bert decided. "Why don't we examine every fireplace in the lodge?"

"All right," said Nan, "but let's take the one nearest my room first."

Bert agreed, so they went into a room next to the wing, where there was a small fireplace. Bert crawled inside it and stood up. He beamed Ben's flashlight around the sooty walls of the chimney while Nan carefully examined the hearth and the stones around the fireplace.

"I don't see anything," Nan said.

"Neither do I," came Bert's muffled voice, "I—ugh!"

Without warning a shower of soot had come down the chimney, covering the boy. He fell to his knees and crawled out. Nan could not help laughing at his funny appearance.

"Bert, you're a sight!" she cried.

She helped brush him off, then took a handkerchief from her pocket so he could wipe his face. She suggested that he go and wash, but Bert said this would take too much time. He was sure that if the gold was not hidden in this fireplace, it was in some other one. He wanted to tackle the next one without delay.

They tried another farther up the corridor, but again were disappointed. Bert was careful this time not to knock any soot off the sides of the chimney and bring down another shower of black powder.

"Nothing here," he reported. "Let's try the lobby next."

The fireplace in the lobby was considerably larger than the other two. This time Bert helped his sister look all around the hearth and the stones that formed the sides and mantel, but all the stones seemed to be firmly in place.

"I'll try the chimney now," said Bert, and stepped inside.

Suddenly the stone floor of the chimney began to slide noiselessly aside. Before Bert could get out, a wide black hole appeared and he plunged down into inky darkness!

CHAPTER XXIV

THE HAPPY DISCOVERY

NAN stood terrified as her twin disappeared down the hole in the fireplace at Horseshoe Lodge.

"Bert! Bert!" she cried frantically.

When he did not answer Nan ran to the corridor. At the top of her voice she yelled for her mother and father and Ben Stillman.

Returning to the fireplace, she called Bert's name again. This time there was a faint answer:

"I'm—I'm not hurt," Bert called.

Nan was relieved. Just the same, Bert had to be rescued. But how?

By this time Mr. and Mrs. Bobbsey were running up the corridor, with Freddie and Flossie close at their heels. Quickly Nan explained what had happened.

"I'll get a ladder," said Mr. Bobbsey.

Mrs. Bobbsey raced to the fireplace and called to her son. He assured her he was all right. He had landed on an earth floor.

"But I've lost the flashlight," Bert complained, "and it's awfully dark down here."

In the excitement the small twins had completely forgotten about the horseshoe they had found. Now, sure that Bert was not hurt, they showed it to the others. Nan took the horseshoe, excitedly turning it over and over.

"Oh, I'm sure this is the one that belongs on the empty nail," she cried. "Let's hang it up and see if it matches the clean spot on the wall."

Hurrying over to the collection, she set the shoe in place. It fitted exactly. Then Nan had an idea. Pressing hard on the horseshoe with her two hands, she waited expectantly. A moment later she could feel something give way. Then came the tearing of the old wallpaper and in a moment the whole section of the wall began to swing back.

Nan stood in wonder as stone steps leading down were revealed. The others hurried to her side and also looked on, speechless.

"Our horseshoe did it!" Freddie cried joyfully.

"Let's hope this stairway leads to where Bert is," said Mrs. Bobbsey.

"I hope so," Mr. Bobbsey, who had returned, agreed. "I couldn't find a ladder."

Mrs. Bobbsey was first to go down the steps. But the others were close behind her. As she reached the bottom step, she saw a soot-covered boy.

"Bert!" Mrs. Bobbsey exclaimed.

Nothing seemed natural about her son except his

voice. He was completely black from head to toe. Blinking through his sooty eyelashes, he cried:

"Those stairs! How did you find them?"

Flossie and Freddie proudly told him how they had found Fiddle's horseshoe, and how it had opened the wall. Then, as Bert brushed the soot from his face, the others looked around to see where they were.

It was a fairly small room with no windows. A narrow iron ladder ran up one of the whitewashed stone walls to the opening in the fireplace through which Bert had fallen.

Suddenly Nan shouted:

"Look! The record player!" She dashed forward to where a table stood in the centre of the room, a portable record player on it.

"And here's the record!" she added, reading the name. "It's *Danse Macabre!*"

"And there's a chimney opening," Bert said excitedly, pointing. "That probably leads right up to your room."

"That's why I heard the violin music so plainly," Nan agreed.

"We've solved that mystery," Bert said, "and we know that whoever brought the record player here must have known how to work the fireplace opening from the top of that ladder. But we still don't know how he got in from outside the building."

"That's right," his father agreed. "Let's look for another entrance to this room."

In their search they noticed that the walls of the room had been badly hacked. Mr. Bobbsey said that probably the intruder had been hunting for the hidden gold. While he had not discovered how to open the wall at the top of the steps, since the wallpaper had not been torn, he had jiggled the horseshoes hanging on the other side of the wall and had made them fall down.

"This looks like a door!" Bert cried suddenly.

All the Bobbseys rushed over to where Bert was playing a flashlight on a section of the outer wall of the room. The old whitewash was plainly cracked in a square outline. There was no handle or knob, but when Mr. Bobbsey and Bert pressed their shoulders to the section, it swung outwards on rusty hinges.

"That's it!" Freddie shouted. "That's the way that bad Will Hemp gets in and out!"

"You're right, son," Mr. Bobbsey agreed, peering out. "This leads out on to the steep hill behind the lodge. It must have been right about here where we found the hat Saturday night."

As the Bobbseys trooped back to the stone stairway, Flossie quoted the words in the riddle:

> " 'To find my gold
> You must be bold.
> My Horseshoes and my Fiddle
> Are the answer to this riddle.' "

"We found the answer, but we didn't find the gold," Freddie complained.

"I wonder if there really is any gold buried here," Bert sighed.

As they reached the foot of the stairway, Nan took the flashlight to make a last investigation of the cellar room. Under the stairway she saw another nail.

"Wait!" she cried. "I want to try something."

Dashing up the stone steps, she took Fiddle's horseshoe from the nail where it still hung. Then she raced back to the nail she had found under the steps. After planting the horseshoe firmly upon it, she pressed on the shoe and waited. This time there was no delay. A small section of the stone-work swung open easily.

Nan beamed her light into the opening and gave a shriek of delight. Reaching in her hand, she tugged at a heavy sack. When she pulled it out, the weight was too much for her and the bag fell to the floor.

Out spilled several gold pieces!

"The gold! The gold!" cried the little twins.

Mr. and Mrs. Bobbsey stared at each other.

"Why, this is a fortune!" the twins' father said, after he leaned down and looked into the sack. "Bundles and bundles of Government bonds that are as good as gold!"

The children gathered up the gold pieces and Mr. Bobbsey carried the sack up the stone steps and over to the wing of the lodge. "I'll get in touch with Mr. Hall at once," he said, and went to telephone.

Ben Stillman was overwhelmed when he heard the news. For once the old man smiled broadly and said he was very glad the inheritance had been found and the mystery solved.

When Mr. Bobbsey told the story to Mr. Hall on the telephone, the banker could hardly believe his ears. He said he would come over at once to take charge of the money.

"My goodness, look what time it is!" Mrs. Bobbsey said. "If we don't hurry, we'll be too late to be in the parade!"

The twins scurried up the stairway. They bathed and changed quickly into clean clothes. When Mr. Hall arrived he insisted that the Bobbseys should be his guests at luncheon.

"But we can't take very much time to eat," said Flossie. "You know we're going to ride in a stage-coach and we have to put on our costumes."

They ate at an hotel but soon returned to Horse-shoe Lodge to put on the special old-fashioned clothes. There was much giggling from the boys' room as they tried to get into the tight trousers and adjust the wigs on their heads.

When everyone was ready, the Bobbsey family gathered in the lower hall. Just as they were about to leave the house, a car pulled up in front of the wing.

"It's Mr. Dickson!" Nan called to the others. "And Dinah's with him."

"How wonderful!" Flossie cried out.

When the newcomers saw the Bobbsey twins in costume, they smiled broadly.

"Why, you look so beautiful," Dinah said, getting out of the car.

"And we feel bee-yoo-ti-ful too!" Flossie cried. "We're going to ride in the stage-coach in the parade, and Mr. Dickson, we've found your gold!"

The young man stared, speechless. He did not know whether to believe the little girl or not.

"It's true," Nan told him. "We found your inheritance and Daddy says it's a fortune."

Tears came to Mr. Dickson's eyes. He could hardly believe the good news.

"You—you found it?" he said. "That's marvellous. Now I can pay my bills and my wife and daughter can have proper medical care. After that I can build a factory and start manufacturing my glue and my glue dissolvent!"

Mr. Bobbsey drove his family to where the stage-coach was standing. Sam was there, ready to help the young folks into the vehicle. They told him about the exciting discovery, then he climbed up into the footman's seat behind them.

Mr. Cowan, in a colourful costume, was seated in the driver's place. Bert climbed up beside him and sat with his arms folded.

Freddie and the girls waved gaily from the

inside, and the coach moved off down the street. It took its place in the long line and soon the parade started.

Such waving and cheering! For a while the Bobbsey twins acted very dignified. But soon they found so many people from Lakeport who had come over for the celebration that they had to wave and smile at them.

"There's Joy and her mother and father," Nan called out, "and Miss Fairweather."

"And there's Danny Rugg," Freddie pointed out. "Boy, does he look mad!"

Danny glowered at the twins as they rode by. He reached his hand into his pocket and for a moment they thought he might be planning to throw a bomb at them. But apparently Danny had learned his lesson, for he pulled his hand out again empty.

Presently the parade halted. As the coach stood waiting, Patrolman Murtry hurried up to the twins.

"Will Hemp has just been captured," he whispered. "Now everybody's worries are over."

"Hurrah!" Freddie shouted.

"Did he confess everything?" Bert called down.

"Yes, he did," the officer replied. "He overheard Mr. Dickson talking about the money he was supposed to get. Hemp figured it was hidden in the old hotel and was determined to find it. Although he wasn't successful in that search, he's the one who took the sapphire from the horseshoe.

"When you Bobbseys arrived, you kind of spoiled his plans, so he decided to try scaring you away by making the place seem haunted. He even brought in the record player and played violin music up the chimney."

"How did he find the secret entrance?" Bert asked the policeman.

"Quite by accident. He was hiding in the bushes on the hill behind the lodge one day, and stepped backwards. He happened to hit the secret door in just the right place."

"And did Will Hemp steal some of Mr. Dickson's glue and the dissolvent?" Nan asked.

"Yes, he admitted doing that, too," replied Patrolman Murtry, and added, "Well, I guess we're all relieved he didn't find the inheritance. And I'm certainly glad you children did."

At this moment the band began to play again and the parade moved on. The policeman waved good-bye to the Bobbseys.

A few minutes later the stage-coach reached the reviewing stand. The mayor stood up and waved his hand for the parade to stop. He bowed to the Bobbseys and then through a loudspeaker said:

"Friends of the 175th anniversary celebration, I want to introduce you all to the Bobbsey twins from Lakeport. They are seated in the stage-coach. Today they did the town of Bartley a great service. They solved the mystery of the old lodge and found a hidden fortune of great value."

"Hurray! Hurray for the Bobbsey twins!" people shouted.

There was great hand-clapping and shouts of congratulation. Then the parade started up again. Far down the street Mr. and Mrs. Bobbsey and Dinah were proudly waiting for the twins. Sam climbed down and assisted his "folks" out of the stage-coach.

"Oh, Dinah, wasn't everything just perfect?" Flossie cried, grabbing her hand. "This is the luckiest day in all our lives."

Dinah smiled. "I expect it is, honey child," she said. "But always remember this: If you work hard to have good luck, you surely won't have bad luck. You all did work hard to solve the mystery, and now you're happy. And happiness is the best kind of good luck."

Read more of the Twins' adventures in
"THE BOBBSEY TWINS AT WHITESAIL HARBOUR"